THE LETTER

Amanda sorted the mail, placing it in the proper mailboxes. One letter was crumpled and mud-splattered, but the familiar, ornate handwriting that had haunted her childhood was unmistakable. It was for Thomas, from Elizabeth in Texas. The flap was open. *What would one peek hurt? The U.S. mail is serious business . . .* The front door opened. Amanda jumped, then quickly stuffed the letter into her pocket.

It was him—Thomas. He approached the counter, smiling. He was taller than she remembered and far more handsome and mature-looking. His dark brown eyes met hers, but she couldn't stand to look for too long. Her knees and voice both shook. "T-T-Thomas."

"It's good to see you again, Amanda."

"It's good to see you, Thomas. Is there something I can get for you?"

"Just my mail."

"Your mail?" Amanda's face felt hot. Her hands fluttered nervously through the pile of letters.

"I—I'm sorry, Thomas, I don't see anything for you right now . . ."

With Love, Amanda

SHELLY RITTHALER

AN AVON FLARE BOOK

WITH LOVE, AMANDA is an original publication of Avon Books. This work has never before appeared in book form.

AVON BOOKS
A division of
The Hearst Corporation
1350 Avenue of the Americas
New York, New York 10019

Copyright © 1997 by Shelly Ritthaler
Published by arrangement with the author
Library of Congress Catalog Card Number: 96-96911
ISBN: 0-380-78375-4
RL: 6.1

First Avon Flare Printing: February 1997

AVON FLARE TRADEMARK REG. U.S. PAT. OFF. AND IN OTHER COUNTRIES, MARCA REGISTRADA, HECHO EN U.S.A.

Printed in the U.S.A.

RA 10 9 8 7 6 5 4 3 2 1

As always, for Reuben and Min Dee, who bring so much to my work and stories. And to the memory of Alice Hillstead Hill, my wonderful grandmother, who didn't enjoy the equality and rights I enjoy today.

Acknowledgments

A special thanks goes to Laila Jagers at the Campbell County Library and to LaVaughn Bresnahan at the Wyoming State Archives for their help with the research for this book. And to Sherri Boothroyd at the Upton, Wyoming, Branch Library. I very much appreciate the fine facilities and services at the Upton Library, the Campbell County Library, and the Wyoming State Archives.

Author's Note

The following characters and the roles they play in this story are not fictitious: Susan B. Anthony, Elizabeth Cady Stanton, Redelia Bates, Colonel William H. Bright, H. G. Nickerson, Ben Sheeks, Esther Morris, and Governor John A. Campbell. Cheyenne and South Pass City, Wyoming Territory, were real cities in 1869. Paradise is a fictitious place and all other characters are fictitious.

Wyoming is the first place on God's green earth which could consistently claim to be the land of the free!

—*Susan B. Anthony, on the passage of the suffrage act in Wyoming Territory, 1871.*

Chapter 1

August 1869

Amanda Chappell shifted in the hard seat as the train
click-clacked west toward Wyoming Territory. She
adjusted her gray cotton traveling suit and thought about
her father with a mixture of dread and anticipation.
Their parting two years ago had not been pleasant, to
say the least. *Had he really forgiven her?* she wondered,
and tried to look out the window at the rolling grass-
lands. Her new acquaintance and traveling companion,
Laura Barnes, slept against the glass, effectively
blocking most of the view.

They had met for the first time just before boarding
the train at the station in Omaha, Nebraska. Amanda's
practice-teaching supervisor at the Omaha Normal
School had arranged for them to travel together. Laura
was on her way to a teaching job in a gold rush town
called South Pass City in central Wyoming Territory.
Amanda, a recent graduate from the teaching school,
was going to her first job at a small town in eastern
Wyoming Territory called Paradise. Laura, who had already taught for two years, acted like an old, experi-

enced hand at teaching. For the first leg of their journey, she had given all kinds of teaching advice.

Amanda stretched her slender frame, trying to un-cramp her long legs. When Laura wasn't sleeping or giving Amanda teaching advice, she was expounding her beliefs in equal rights for women and women's suf-frage. She talked endlessly about the speeches of fa-mous suffragettes like Susan B. Anthony, Elizabeth Cady Stanton, and Redelia Bates. Amanda had listened with patience and interest, but her mind was otherwise occupied. She was nervous about her new job and even more anxious about seeing her father again.

Laura opened her blue eyes, smoothed back her blonde hair, sat up, and asked, "Are you all right, Amanda? You look peaked."

Amanda nodded and tried not to think about her fa-ther. Her last, parting words to him, in a tearful, scream-ing rage, had been, "I hate you. I will never, ever, forgive you." The memory made her stomach lurch. She jumped from her seat, ran toward the back of the passenger car and out the door where she stood on the outside platform between the cars. The wind tossed her long, auburn curls and made her hazel eyes water. Tak-ing a deep, cleansing breath, she exhaled and hoped to banish the haunting thoughts into the breeze.

Laura followed Amanda and reached to steady her. Offering a lace-edged handkerchief and raising her voice above the racket of the metal wheels against the iron rails, she asked, "What on earth is wrong? It seems like the closer we get to Wyoming, the more fidgety and upset you get. Your face is pale as a sheet. Surely you're not *this* nervous about your first teaching job. Is it something else? If it is, you better talk about it, so you don't throw yourself off the train before we get there."

"I'm all right," Amanda said, taking the handkerchief and wiping her eyes. The swirling wind made them tear again.

"What could be so terrible? You didn't murder someone or rob a bank? Did you kiss someone's husband?" Laura asked, teasing.

"No, no, no." Amanda laughed and dabbed at her eyes again.

"What, then?"

Amanda took a deep breath and said, "Two years ago, when I last saw my father, I said some terrible, awful things to him. Today will be the first time I've seen him since then."

"Let's go inside so I can hear you," Laura shouted.

They made their way back to their seat. Laura said, "I do talk a lot, but I'm a good listener, as well."

Amanda got the seat beside the window this time. Sitting, she took a minute to decide if she should tell everything or not, and thought about Thomas Lewellen. Immediately, his handsome, dark features flashed in her mind so vividly, it seemed like he stood before her. Her stomach gave a sharp twist. Amanda was disappointed in herself. *After all this time*, she thought, *does he still have the power to affect me, just by thinking about him? I have worked so hard to get over that silly girlhood crush.* Amanda decided the part of the story about him would be too painful to talk about, and chose not to, saying, "Five years ago, when I was eleven years old, my father, mother, and I were living in Omaha. My father, William, and his brother, Philip, were in the mercantile business together. That year, my mother took sick and died."

Laura put her fingers to her lips and whispered, "I'm so sorry."

"We took it real hard," Amanda continued. "Father decided he needed to get away from the memories of my mother. At the same time, the Union Pacific was

3

starting an incredible venture. They were building a transcontinental railroad to join the west coast to the east coast for the first time. In fact, the tracks we're traveling on right now are the very tracks they were building then. My father was taken with that vision. He'd say to me, 'Imagine, a railroad joining the two ends of this great big country. They're going to connect California to Omaha and the rest of the country with rails.' At that time, the rails from the east coast reached Omaha, but didn't go any farther west. My father said, 'When the railroad is finished, people will be able to travel from one end of America to the other in just a few days. I want to be a part of building that dream.' "

"Did he go to work for the railroad?" Laura asked.

"No, not exactly. We loaded a big wagon with groceries, supplies, and a huge canvas tent. Away we went, chasing the railroad. We hooked up with the graders crew and followed along with them, selling groceries and supplies as we went."

"I don't know much about railroads," Laura said. "What is a graders crew?"

"The graders were the workers who built the railroad grade, or bed. They graded it with fresnos pulled by horses to flatten it and make it even. That's why they were called graders. When they finished one part of the grade, they moved on up the line to make way for the track layers who followed, setting the ties and laying the rails. Even though my father didn't actually build the railroad, we were still a part of it, traveling with the crews, living like gypsies and selling groceries and supplies out of our tent.

"Where did you live?" Laura asked.

"In the tent. It was the store and our home. Every week or so, my uncle Philip drove out to meet us with another wagon filled with fresh supplies and groceries. He left the new wagon and took the empty one back to

4

Omaha to refill it and bring it back again. As the grader crew moved west, so did we, packing up the tent and inventory, moving on and setting it up, moving on and setting it up, over and over, in a frenzy of moving and building. Sometimes, when we'd get a new shipment of supplies, people couldn't wait for us to unload the wagon. They demanded we open the crates and sell things right out of the back of the wagon.''

"Did you like it?"

"I liked it a lot. There was another family in the camp, the Hendersons. They took my father, me, and a young man named Thomas Lewellen. . . ." Amanda caught herself, surprised at the way her heart thumped and picked up its pace when she mentioned his name. "They took us in, and we were like one big family. Jacob Henderson is a very good carpenter. He was in charge of building bridges and trestles. He and his wife, Claire, who was my guardian angel, have seven children. Their children were like my brothers and sisters. Claire kept me and all of her children from turning into a bunch of wild little heathens. She made us sit down every day to do lessons and taught us penmanship, arithmetic, reading, and manners. The only textbook we had was her big, family Bible, so we learned to read using it. If we worked hard on our chores and lessons, she let us have our afternoons to run free. When the weather was good, we got together with the other children in the camp and played baseball."

"Girls and boys together? You all played baseball?" Laura's mouth dropped open.

"Girls, boys, it didn't make any difference. We had to have both, or we wouldn't have enough people for two teams. We girls just hitched up our skirts, tied them with pieces of rope, and played right along with the boys. No one thought anything of it."

Laura's eyes popped wide, as she said, "That's wonderfully defiant and equal. It appeals to all my suffragette beliefs.''

Amanda couldn't help smiling, and hoped Laura wouldn't start talking about women getting the right to vote and women's equal rights again.

"What happened with your father?" Laura asked, getting back to the story. "What was your big fight about?"

"For three years, that's how we lived. It was like a camping trip or adventure that never ended. When I was fourteen years old, we were getting close to where Cheyenne, Wyoming Territory is located today. I was in the tent by myself, watching over things while my father went to get some water. A man who worked on the crew, I didn't know his name, came into the tent and asked if we had gloves. I went to get some for him. He followed me real close and smelled like dirty sweat and whiskey. He said I was a pretty thing, and maybe we should get married. I tried to move away from him, but he grabbed me and tried to kiss me. Just then, my father came in and yelled, 'Hey! That's my daughter.' Father was so angry. He grabbed the man, shook him, and told him to get outside, get some air, sober up, and don't come back. I thought he was going to tear off his head.''

"How terrible. Were you scared?"

"It happened too fast for me to be scared."

"What did they do to the man? Did they run him out of camp?"

"I don't know. The next morning, my uncle Philip arrived with a wagon full of fresh supplies. When he got ready to return to Omaha that afternoon, two twelve-year-old little girls, me, and all of our belongings were loaded in the back of his empty wagon. We were being sent back to Omaha with Uncle Philip. When I figured out what was happening, and that we were being

6

sent away, I lost my temper. That's what the fight was about. I was in the back of that wagon crying and beating my feet and fists against the wagon bed, screaming, 'I will never, ever forgive you.' My father turned and walked away. That was the last time I saw him as we drove away from the camp. The other little girls had relatives in Omaha. They went to live with them, and I went to live with my aunt and uncle.''

"I don't blame you for being mad," Laura interrupted. "I would have been angry, too."

Amanda shrugged. "Now that I'm a little older, I can see why they sent us away. The camp was full of rough, unmarried men. At times, it got pretty rowdy. Now, I realize my father and the parents of the other little girls just wanted to protect us. But it was hard to see that at the time."

"I would have thrown a fit, too."

"My mother was part Irish, and my father says I inherited her red hair, her eye color, and her quick, fierce temper." Remembering, Amanda smiled. "That day, everyone saw the full fury of my inherited temper. Leaving my father, the Hendersons, and their children was like losing my family, just like I lost my mother.

"While I was in Omaha, my aunt and uncle were very good to me. I had the chance to finish school, then go through normal school to earn my teaching certificate. For that, I'm grateful, but I never quit missing my father and the Hendersons." *And Thomas,* Amanda thought, *the one I swore I would never quit loving. He was the hardest one to leave. That's what I was really angry about then. I didn't want to be taken away from him. But now, thank heaven that's all in the past.*

"You've written to your father since then, haven't you?" Laura asked.

"He wrote to me all the time. For a long time, I refused to write to him, but eventually, I did. Then we

7

wrote regularly. In one letter, I begged forgiveness for my behavior that day. He wrote and said all was forgiven, and we never mentioned it again. From our letters, it seems like things are good between us. But I don't know for sure. Father and the Hendersons went on with the railroad crews to Promatory Summit in Utah. That's where the track coming from the west met our track from the east. They were there last May, when they drove the two golden and the two silver spikes into the track when the two ends joined. I wish I had been there to see history being made. I still feel cheated because I wasn't.''

"That is what I keep talking about," Laura said, her voice full of fire and vinegar. "Life is so unfair to girls and women. They should have tied that evil man to the back end of a fast horse and dragged him away. He's the one who should have been punished. We live in a man's world, Amanda. Men rule it. They always have. As women, we need a collective voice starting now, today. We must fight to get the right to vote, to own our own property, and to get equal pay for doing the same work men do.''

Amanda shifted in the seat and said, "Laura, I believe in this cause and want to help you with it. But for today, I just want to see my father and make sure things are all right between us.''

"How come your father stayed in Wyoming Territory when the railroad was finished?" Laura asked, trying to calm her voice after her outburst.

"The Union Pacific Railroad people approached my father and Mr. Henderson and told them they needed to establish a train station and a town about forty miles east of Cheyenne. They needed a station at approximately that location to resupply the steam locomotives with fresh water and wood so they could travel on up the track. The Union Pacific offered my father and

Jacob free land if they would start a new town. So they did, and called it Paradise. Since then, several other families and businesses have moved in, and right now, as we speak, they should almost be done building the new school. When they started planning and building it, they offered me the teaching position. I accepted, finished my teacher's training, and now, here I am with you, on my way to my new job and my old family.'' Amanda thought, *and a fresh start without silly childish infatuations that mean nothing.* She sighed, then wanting to change the subject, asked, ''Are you nervous about your job in South Pass City?''

Laura was eighteen, two years older than Amanda. She stretched like a sleek, contented cat, and said, ''Not a bit. South Pass is perfect for me. I want adventure and excitement. I don't want to be a tea-parlor lady, or a diaper-changing drudge. Give me the wild frontier, freedom, equal rights, and the right to vote. It's a revolution. We owe it to women everywhere in the world to bear the standard, hold it high, and never let down our resolve to fight for the equality of women. Enough of this *man's* world. It's women like us who are going to change things, Amanda, you and me. Young, single women like us should all promise never to marry until we can be equal partners in our marriages. If we would all do that, we'd get the right to vote sooner.''

It was only the fifth or sixth time on the trip that Laura had repeated her call-to-the-revolution-for-women speech. Amanda smiled to herself, half listened, and nodded her head or shook it in all the proper places as Laura talked. She could guess exactly how Laura would react if she were to tell her the truth about Thomas Lewellen. Amanda didn't need Laura or anyone else to tell her what an immature fool she had been. She had told herself that enough times in the past two years.

''Before we get to Paradise, we should make a pact,''

Laura proposed with a glint in her eye. "Let's promise each other we will never fall in love or marry until we have the right to vote and equal rights guaranteed under the law. Let's promise to do everything we can to change the world."

"Are you serious, Laura?"

"Completely serious. You're not afraid to change the world, are you?"

"No." Amanda's eyes widened in surprise as Laura thrust out her hand.

"Then shake on it," she dared.

Amanda stared at the hand. The words began to sink into an inner part of her heart. Laura had made it perfectly clear that she hated men. As she said, "To fall in love is a betrayal to the cause of women and equal rights," Amanda remembered her past feelings for Thomas. They had been feelings over which she had no control and that had never been returned. She told herself with an embarrassed blush, *A fourteen-year-old girl isn't capable of being in true and lasting love. My feelings for Thomas were just childish infatuations, puppy love. Now, I'm more than ready to move on to other passions.* The idea of working to change the world had an appealing ring to it. Amanda wanted to change the world, even if it was a small part of it. She wanted to mark her place in history, especially if it meant making the world a better place for all women. Taking Laura's hand, she gave it a firm shake.

"This is a solemn oath," Laura warned.

"Here's to changing the world," Amanda said, confirming her friend's resolve.

The uniformed conductor entered their passenger car and called, "Next stop, Paradise, Wyoming Territory."

Chapter 2

Searching the scenery passing by the window, Amanda looked for the town, her anticipation building. To the north and west she saw a backdrop of steep, blue-tinted mountains. A two-story frame building with a black and white sign hanging on its side grew larger in the corner of the window. The sign said PARADISE. The train slowed. The breaks squealed. Paradise was surrounded by a scattering of massive, gnarled cottonwood trees and open grassland dotted with sagebrush.

On the station platform stood her father, William Chappell, tall, angular, and balding. Next to him was stout, robust Jacob Henderson and seven children of different sizes. They all anxiously searched the train windows, looking for her. Amanda, unable to wait any longer, jumped from her seat, piled over Laura in an unladylike manner, and ran to the door. The conductor blocked her way, holding her until the train stopped. She jerked away from him, opened the door, shouted, and waved her arms. "Father, here I am! Here I am!"

"Amanda!" William Chappell yelled, running toward her, his arms outstretched. Amanda jumped from the steps into his arms. "Amanda. My dear girl," he whis-

11

pered, holding her so tight she could hardly breathe. "Welcome home." He spun her around and set her on the platform. Jacob and the children rushed about her, struggling to get close.

Amanda nervously laughed and tried to gather them all in her arms. Even though she hadn't seen a house, or the town itself, she knew, standing in their arms, that she was home, the place she had longed to be for the past two years.

"Amanda?" Laura interrupted them. "Here's your carpetbag." She set it on the platform.

Amanda pulled away from them and said, "Everyone, I want you to meet my new friend and traveling companion, Laura Barnes. Laura is going to Cheyenne, then on to South Pass City. Laura, this is my father, William. This is my other father, Jacob Henderson."

Amanda was grateful when Jacob gave Laura's hand a hearty shake and introduced the children. They had grown and changed like weeds in a garden in the past two years, and she wasn't sure she'd get all of their names placed with the right faces.

Jacob said, "This is David, he's the oldest, he's eleven. Ezekiel, we call him Zeek, is ten. Jeremiah and Samuel are twins, and nine years old. Ruth, with her million freckles, is seven. Joseph, with the missing front teeth, is six, and last but not least, is four-year-old Leah."

"Where is Claire?" Amanda asked, searching the platform for Jacob's wife.

"She's at the mercantile all full of secrets and surprises for you." William laughed.

The train conductor called, "All aboard for Cheyenne."

"I best get on the train," Laura said, her voice nervous. "They'll leave me."

12

Amanda hugged her and said, "Good-bye, friend. Write to me."

"I will. Don't forget our promise to change the world."

Laura climbed aboard the train and waved before ducking inside the car. Amanda blew her a kiss, then put an arm around her tall father. Jacob Henderson, with his thick muscular arms, took her carpetbag and introduced her to the stationmaster, Robert Hunter. Jacob told him they would bring a wagon for her luggage later. The portly Mr. Hunter, with his walrus-like mustache, shook Amanda's hand and said, "Nice to meet you," and waved them off without another word. They walked up the street toward the mercantile. The children gathered close to Amanda, each trying to hold on to her hands. They gently pushed and shoved each other as they walked. Amanda tried to hold all of the children's hands, and wondered why she had been so apprehensive about seeing them all again. Her father described the different buildings as they moved up the street. The buildings were neat wooden structures with wood-shake shingles. On the right side of the street was the livery barn and blacksmith shop, then the feed and grain store. Last was the saloon. On the left was the train station, with its tall, round, wooden water tower, and the station house surrounded by a wooden platform. Next was a small two-story hotel and boarding house. Then came a combination bank and land office, followed by Amanda's father's mercantile. There were two main streets, the one they were walking up, which ran north and south until it formed a T intersection with the other street, running east and west on the other side of the mercantile. At the top of the intersection of the two streets sat the new, white school building.

"Not far from the school, down that road to the east, is Jacob's sawmill and carpentry shop," her father explained. Scattered among the cottonwood trees and radiating out from the heart of the town, Amanda could see several homes. "Behind the school and those trees is the creek," he added. "Not a lot of people live here yet. The town is only a few months old, but give us a little time, and we'll grow, just wait and see. Most everyone here works for the railroad or at Jacob's sawmill making firewood for the locomotives and lumber to ship on the cars."

The children were pushing each other a little harder to get closer to Amanda.

"We have about twelve families, three with children old enough to go to school. . . ."

"That's us," one of the children shouted and shoved another child, almost tripping Amanda.

"Hey," Jacob said in a stern voice. "You younguns go up to the spring and fetch that jug of buttermilk like your Ma asked."

"All of us?" four-year-old Ruth asked, a whine in her voice.

"All of you. Go. Run and get rid of all this energy so you'll be ready to sit in the house and talk quietlike. Go."

The children ran up the street shouting, laughing, and still pushing at each other as Amanda and the two men stopped in front of the mercantile. It was a sturdy two-story building with a false board front. Painted on it, in huge ornate red and black letters, were the words, *Chappell's Mercantile*. "What do you think?" her father asked.

"It's beautiful," Amanda exclaimed. "You only came here in May. It's August now. How did all of this get done so fast?"

William and Jacob laughed. "Hard work," Jacob said.

"We've been working night and day," William said.

"Part of it was fairly easy. After the railroad construction crews moved out of Cheyenne and down the track, many of the people moved on, too, leaving several empty buildings. We were able to buy some of them very cheap and dismantle them. The Union Pacific brought them here, in pieces, on flat cars. We simply put them together again. The school, the sawmill, a few homes, the livery barn, and the train station are brand-new buildings. The rest are reconstructed."

"Thank goodness, otherwise we'd still be building like mad, living in tents, and praying the snow doesn't come too soon," Jacob said.

"We still have a lot of work to do, but we've come a long way. Take a look," William said and stepped up to the door, opened it, and bending his angular frame into a grand bow, ushered her into the mercantile.

Amanda's eyes nearly popped when she saw the ceiling-high shelves neatly lined with tins, goods, and supplies of all kinds. A carved oak counter skirted the right wall and part of the back wall. On the back wall, behind the counter, she could see the little box-like compartments that served as mailboxes. On the left wall was a potbellied stove surrounded by a few wooden chairs and a small table with a checkerboard on it. "It's beautiful, Father!" Amanda exclaimed.

"Come upstairs. Claire has a surprise for us," William said, holding her hand.

They trooped behind the counter, through the cloth curtains, into the backroom and up the inside staircase. The second story was divided into two separate halves. One half was split into four bright rooms which made up a comfortable living area. There were two bedrooms, a small kitchen, and a sitting room. The rooms were furnished with sparse but functional furniture, a sofa, beds, dressers, tables, and chairs. Separated from the living area, a door opened into a huge, unfinished storeroom with its own doorway leading to another, outside staircase. Her father was using the storage space for carryover goods and extra stock for the mercantile.

"I'm not much of a decorator," her father said as he showed her around. "I waited to let you do that. Fix it up however you like. Maybe it'll be a little nicer then. I'm so glad you're here. I'm going to have to ask you for your help in the store for a few weeks because I want to dig a fairly large root cellar. I'll need your help while I do that, if you don't mind."

Amanda could see that the rooms needed vases and curtains, wallpaper, doilies, and other touches to make them more inviting. "Count on me," she said, giving his hand a squeeze.

"Let's see what Claire has for us," he urged.

Amanda went into the kitchen. Claire Henderson was taking two large sour-cream raisin pies from a basket and setting them on the table. Amanda put her arms around Claire's slim, graceful frame and said, "Those look wonderful, and so do you."

"Welcome home, sweetheart," Claire said, enfolding Amanda in her arms and holding her close for a long time. "I made your favorite pies," she said, making Amanda stand an arm's-length away so she could study her clear complexion and hourglass figure. "Goodness gracious, we sent a little girl to Omaha, and what did we get back? A beautiful young lady. My, how you have grown up and changed."

Amanda blushed and looked fondly at Claire's graying hair pulled into a tight bun and her clear, brown eyes. "Do you really think so, Claire?"

"I wouldn't say so, if I didn't think so," Claire stated in her matter-of-fact way. Amanda smiled to herself. Claire hadn't changed her no fuss, no frills manner one bit.

They heard the children clattering up the stairs, and

Claire filled the plates with thick slabs of creamy pie. "This is a wonderful welcome," Amanda told her. "Thank you, Claire."

"We're so glad you're home."

Jeremiah and Samuel set the crockery jug of buttermilk on the table, and Claire hushed the children's chattering with a stern look. "Go, sit down, and we'll eat," she said. The children scurried without a single word.

Soon they were all gathered, adults in chairs, the seven children seated on the floor of the sitting room. They visited companionably and filled themselves with cool buttermilk and sweet pie until no one could eat any more.

When the evening shadows lengthened, Jacob sent the two oldest boys, David and Zeek, to hitch up the wagon and go to the station for Amanda's trunk and other luggage. After they returned and set Amanda's things in her room, the Henderson family climbed aboard the wagon and drove up the street. Amanda and her father stood arm in arm on the boardwalk in front of the mercantile and waved until the wagon turned east and disappeared into the trees and shadows.

The next day, Amanda spent the morning helping her father in the store. She waited on customers and acquainted herself with the local residents, most of whom worked for the Union Pacific Railroad. At noon she started at the front of the store with a feather duster, dusting the shelves and restocking them as she went. By late afternoon, she had worked her way to the back of the store to the mailboxes. As she dusted the square, box-like compartments, she paused to study the names that were pasted on each slot. *Anderson, Baker, Chappell, Henderson, Hunter, Lewellen, McClain . . .* Amanda's heart skipped a beat. *Lewellen? It can't be.* She looked a second time and caught her breath. *Surely not.* Amanda swallowed and made sure she had control of her voice before she said, "Father, I see a postal box here for Lewellen." Her hands shook. She shoved them in her apron pockets. "That doesn't happen to be Thomas Lewellen, does it?"

"Sure is," William said, coming from the back room with a crate of canned peaches. "You remember him, don't you?"

Amanda's heart pounded so hard, her head hurt. Her voice quivered slightly. "The very same Thomas Lewellen who worked on the grader crew?"

"One and the same." William unpacked the canned peaches, stacking them in a display by the cracker barrel in the center of the floor. "Is everything all right?" he asked, stopping his work.

"Fine." Amanda faked a laugh. "I'm surprised to find Thomas here. It's like I never left at all. The whole family is here in Paradise."

"It's nice, isn't it?" William said, and the bell above the front door tinkled. Before Amanda could answer him, he went to wait on the customer.

Amanda held the edge of the counter to steady herself. *Nice depends on your point of view,* she thought, and told herself, *If I had known he was here, I never, never would have come here, too.*

Hours later, she finished the day, her feelings a dreary, miserable haze. That evening at supper, her father watched her, concern filling his face. "Are you all right? You've been terribly quiet all afternoon."

"I'm just more tired from the trip than I thought I would be, and I'm nervous about teaching school for the first time."

"I can understand that." He reached for her hand. "The Hendersons and I wanted to surprise you and wait until the school was completely finished before we showed it to you. But why don't you go over there tomorrow and take a look around. See if it meets your approval. Now off to bed. I shouldn't have let you do anything today. You should have rested."

"Father, I'm fine."

"Off to bed. I'll put up the dishes. Get some sleep. Tomorrow you can inspect your new school."

Amanda kissed him on the top of his balding head and went to her room. She brushed her long hair, braided it, dressed in a cotton nightgown, and climbed into bed. Her mind filled with painful memories. She was transported back in time to when she was twelve years old. She and the other children had been playing baseball. Her skirts were grass-stained and her auburn braids were a loose, ratty mess. She sneaked into the tent-store to get some candy for herself and her friends. While she had her hand deep in the horehound jar, Thomas Lewellen, with his southern drawl, dark hair, and the smooth cheeks of a fifteen-year-old, quietly came into the tent and stood watching her. When Amanda looked up, something happened to her. The air left her lungs, her heart thumped, and she couldn't take her eyes from him. "D-do you want a piece of horehound?" she stammered. "It's free."

He took a piece from her, popped it into his mouth, and asked if she knew where to find Jacob Henderson. Amanda told him. He thanked her and left. That day, Thomas went to work assisting Jacob on the crew. The Hendersons and her father made him a part of their families' social events and numerous meals. *My life changed that day,* Amanda told herself. *I fell in love, or, what I thought was love at the time, but he didn't.* She remembered how terrible it felt to be a little girl who suddenly and desperately needed to be a woman. But her body hadn't cooperated. She still looked like a little girl and felt that way except for when she was around him. Whenever she could, she followed him about like a confused, love-sick puppy. He was always friendly and kind to her. Once in a while, whenever he got a break from his railroad work, he joined her and the other children in a game of baseball. But he never treated Amanda any different than he treated any of the other children. Amanda had no idea how she wanted to be treated, but it certainly wasn't like the rest of the children. Somehow, she wanted to be special to the young Texan.

From the time she was twelve until she was fourteen years old, Amanda found herself constantly praying that some wonderful, magical event would immediately transform her into a graceful, gorgeous woman with charms he couldn't help but notice and couldn't resist. Then, one Sunday, after two years of secretly yearning, she put on her best dress, undid her long braids, brushed her hair into a curly, red mass, and went to find him. He was sitting next to a creek under a box elder tree. Amanda sat beside him, told him that she loved him, and asked him to marry her.

The memory made Amanda's face and chest grow hot. She climbed out of bed and opened the windows as wide as they would go. The air surrounding the quiet, dark street was hot and stifling. Amanda studied the twinkling stars, fixed her gaze on the brightest one, and whispered, "Star light, star bright, first star I see tonight, I wish I may, I wish I might, have my first wish tonight. I wish—no I don't wish—I beg you, please, please, save me from ever making a fool of myself like that again."

Amanda crawled into bed, cast the sheets and quilt aside, and hugged her pillow. Thomas had been so kind then. After she'd asked him to marry her, he'd told her that if he was of a mind to be getting married, and if they were both a lot older, her offer was certainly one he would consider. He said, "I'm very flattered. Thank you for asking me, though. When I'm ready, I'll think about it. But it may be a very long, long time."

"I don't care, I love you," she'd told him.

He'd leaned close. She still remembered his clean, musky scent. He'd lifted her chin with the tip of his thumb and said, "Amanda, we both have some growing up to do. I have some things I have to work out in my mind and life. When you get grown-up, you probably won't feel this way about me. You will probably love several boys and young men before you give your heart to one man. And he will be very lucky. You are sweet, Amanda, so very sweet." He gently brushed her hair away from her forehead and kissed it.

Amanda's little heart nearly burst wide open. She jumped up and, running away from him, called, "I'll wait for you, Thomas. I'll wait forever." As she had run back to camp, her heart had soared. She'd memorized the feel of his lips on her forehead, not realizing it would be the last time in a long time that she would see him. When she had arrived breathless at the tent, her father asked her to look after things while he went to get some water. That's when the drunk man had arrived and tried to kiss her. The next day, she was sent, in a bitter rage, to Omaha in the back of her uncle's wagon.

The kicking, crying, screaming tantrum didn't have as much to do with being sent away as it did with the fact that she couldn't possibly go away then because she had to be there when she suddenly became older and Thomas could give her an answer to her proposal. How would Thomas ever fall in love with her if she wasn't there when she turned 'older'? That was the thing she couldn't forgive, at the time.

In the two years she was in Omaha, Amanda realized how foolish she had been. Time transformed her from a little girl who loved baseball, horehound, and Thomas

21

Lewellen, into a young woman, qualified to teach, who still loved baseball and candy. But since then, she had counted Thomas Lewellen out of her heart and feelings. She involved herself in school and several social circles. Young men had called on her, and while they were interesting and fun, none of them made her heart jump. Not like Thomas had.

Amanda whispered to the ceiling, "I hope you remember that I was just a little girl and forgive all that foolishness, Thomas. I tried to forget you. I really did. But why do you have to be here?" Hot tears pooled in her eyes and dripped from the side of her face onto the pillow.

Chapter 3

Amanda buffed the brass coat hooks with her sleeve, then finished sweeping the sawdust from the unfinished wooden floor of the cloakroom. She stood in the door between the cloakroom and schoolroom, surveying the empty building. The slate chalkboard hung on the wall. In a couple of days, the desks would be finished and set in place. She sighed, leaned on the broom, and thought, *This is my school, my brand-new school. Will I be a good teacher? Will my students like me and learn from me?*

A locomotive whistle sounded two short toots that echoed in the empty room. Startled, Amanda gasped, let the broom fall to the floor, and fled the empty school. "Oh, no, oh, no," she said, clutching her calico skirt, jumping from the steps and running full-steam down the dusty street. Sweat dotted her brow as she flew in the door of Chappell's Mercantile. She grabbed the canvas mail sack from behind the counter, turned, and flew out the door, leaving it open behind her. Again, two short blasts sounded from the locomotive as she ran toward the station clutching the mail sack. Mr. Hunter, the stationmaster, stood outside the depot, watching her run up the street. The locomotive started to pull out of the station. *No, please wait,* she silently pleaded, and ran harder. Mr. Hunter held a pocket watch attached to his vest by a long fob. He tapped his foot as Amanda rushed toward him. "I'm sorry, Mr. Hunter," she panted.

"We're holding up the train." His bushy, walrus-like mustache bobbed as he spoke. He grabbed the sack from her and hurried to stand by the tracks as the cars clicked past him faster and faster. As the caboose approached, he held the sack aloft. A tall, uniformed conductor stood on the caboose steps, reached, caught the sack, and swung it aboard as the train gained momentum then chugged east away from the station.

Amanda wiped her brow. "I'm sorry, Mr. Hunter, I was working up at the new school and didn't pay attention to the time."

Mr. Hunter cleared his throat and stated, "The U.S. mail is serious business, Miss Chappell."

"Yes, sir, I know."

"I'll get your mail for you."

Amanda followed him into the station house.

"Are they going to have that school ready by next week?" Mr. Hunter asked in a gruff manner. He reached behind the counter and pulled out a canvas sack similar to the one they had just put on the train.

"It's almost done. We need to oil the floors and finish the desks. Then we'll be ready to open." She took the mail sack from him, went to the door, and paused, saying, "I'm sorry I was late."

"Don't ever forget, the U.S. mail is serious business," he said, turning to work at his desk. On the counter next to his desk, a telegraph key click-clicked a merry tune.

Amanda slipped out the door and into the muggy heat. The humidity made her long, auburn hair pull itself into tight unruly kinks and curls. A wagon rattled to a stop next to her.

"Hello, Amanda," said the wagon driver, Jacob Henderson.

"Hello, Jacob."

"Hop up, I'll give you a ride to the mercantile."

Although it wasn't far, Amanda hitched up her calico skirt, climbed aboard, and settled on the wooden seat beside him. "Thanks," she said.

"I heard the locomotive whistle two extra times. . . ."

"It was for me," Amanda admitted, feeling a blush creep up her hot neck. "I was at the school, lost track of time, and almost missed getting the outgoing mail onto the train. Mr. Hunter wasn't very pleased with me."

Jacob patted her knee with his rough, muscular hand, saying, "Don't worry about that old goat." He slapped the reins on the bay horse's rump, and the wagon slowly rolled forward. "You've been here three days, now, what do you think of our little town?"

Amanda praised it, saying, "It's wonderful, Mr. Henderson. I can't believe you built most of these buildings in such a short time."

"We didn't help build the saloon and livery. Cal Taneman, a real old goat, built them. He didn't take any advice from me. Look there . . ." He turned in the seat. Amanda's eyes followed his gaze. "See the roof on the livery barn? It's not quite square. It'll sag before spring. Then he'll want me to help him fix it before it falls in around his ears. I tried to tell him it wasn't square when he built it, but he didn't want to hear about it from me. No, sir. Amanda, you remember something, it's much easier to build it square and true to start with than it is to go back and try to fix it later. That's always been my guiding rule, and not just in building things."

Amanda squinted her eyes, studied the roof line, and tried to see what he was talking about. She didn't want to say so, but it looked straight to her. Jacob continued, "Between me, your father, Thomas, and some of the Union Pacific crew, we built nearly all these other buildings."

"Thomas? Thomas Lewellen?" Amanda tried to act nonchalant and half interested. Her heart skipped a beat. She hoped that by pretending she didn't already know he was there, Jacob would tell her more than she knew.

"Of course Thomas Lewellen, what other Thomas do we know? He's here, working with me in the sawmill and helping me do some building. He built a real nice log house west of the school near the creek."

"I see." Amanda nearly choked on the words. "A house? He must be planning on staying here, then?" Her heart raced.

"I don't know. You know how quiet he is. Never talks much about himself, or any of his doings. He's always been that way." Jacob pulled the wagon to a stop in front of the mercantile. "Here you are, Miss Amanda."

"Thanks, Jacob."

"Anytime. I best get back to the sawmill." Amanda stepped from the wagon and carried the mail sack into the mercantile. She put it on the rear counter, then went up the inside stairs. Her father was in the storeroom shuffling crates here and there, rearranging and organizing things.

"Hello, Father, what are you doing?"

"With the new freight we received today, I finally have no choice but to take some time to get this place organized like I want it. I've stacked the seasonal goods over there, and the things we'll use more often, closer to the door. I'm starting to get some of the winter goods shipped in, but it'll be a while before customers want them. They're over there." He pointed to a neat stack of crates.

"It looks nice."

"I heard the train whistle a couple of extra times. Was there something wrong at the station?"

Amanda had hoped he hadn't heard. Earlier that morning, she'd promised to get the mail to the train station and almost didn't keep her promise. "I stayed a bit long at the school and was late getting the mail to the train. I made it, though, the mail went out. I'm sorry I was late." Her voice rushed on before he could comment or chastise her. "The school is very nice. I'll enjoy teaching in it. You and Jacob did a great job."

The service bell on the counter downstairs pinged. "I'll see to it," Amanda said, and rushed down the stairs. In front of the counter stood the three smallest Henderson children, seven-year-old Ruth, six-year-old Joseph, and petite, four-year-old Leah. Joseph reached up on tiptoe and pinged the small bell again. They giggled. Amanda ducked behind the counter, out of sight, and waited until they reached for the bell a third time. When they did, she jumped up and in a gruff voice yelled, "Hey, what do you want?" The children squealed and grabbed each other, giggling with delight.

"Amanda, you scared us. Don't do that," the littlest ones complained.

Amanda hurried around the counter and opened her arms. The three hurried to snuggle next to her. "We missed you so much, when you were gone," Ruth admitted.

"Are you going away again?" Joseph asked.

"No. I'm here to stay. I'm going be your teacher."

"We know," Joseph added. "Mama says we have to call you Miss Amanda or Miss Chappell at school. Is that what we're supposed to do?"

"If that's what your mama says, that's what we better do."

"How come?" Ruth asked, her arms tight around Amanda's neck.

"It has to do with my being your teacher, now. I think it has to do with me getting older and growing up, too."

"I don't want you to grow up, Amanda," Ruth whispered and snuggled her freckled nose into Amanda's shoulder.

"I want to grow up," Leah insisted. "Mama says I'm too young to go to school. But I'm going anyhow. I am not staying home by myself."

"You won't be home by yourself," Joseph retorted. "Mama will be there."

"I'm not staying home with Mama." Leah stamped her foot.

"We wanted to come see you again, the next day after you got home," Ruth told her, "but Mama said we had to give you time to get rested and settled in. Are you settled in?"

"I am, and I'm glad to see you." Amanda gave them all a squeeze. "You're all getting so big. How are David, Zeek, Jeremiah, and Samuel today?"

"They're fine," Joseph said, then ordered, "show her what we have, Leah."

Leah opened her hand and revealed a penny. "Oh, my goodness," Amanda said, her eyes getting wide with surprise. "Where did you get that?"

"We picked up wood chips and sticks in the sawmill yard for Thomas. He promised us a penny if we would do that. Do you remember Thomas?" Ruth asked.

Amanda's stomach cramped. Did she ever remember Thomas. She never seemed to be able to forget him. She smiled and said, "Of course I remember Thomas. I'm surprised he's here in Paradise, though."

"Where else would he be?" Joseph asked.

"I don't know," Amanda said, and wanting to change the subject, looked around, saying, "Let's see, what can you buy with a penny? Let's see . . ." Amanda studied the stacks of canned goods, tins, ribbons, barrels of bulk goods, and bolts of fabric. She purposely avoided looking at the glass canisters filled with candy along the edge of the counter. "Let me see, for a penny, a penny. We have shoelaces, ribbons, nails. Would you like some nails?"

"You know what we want," Joseph insisted.

"And what would that be?" Amanda put her hands on her hips and acted like she didn't have a clue.

"Amanda! We want candy, candy, candy," Leah insisted, tugging on Amanda's skirt.

"Candy, candy, candy?" Amanda laughed, stepped behind the counter, and put one of the long, white butcher aprons over her head and tied it at her waist. "What kind of candy? Peppermints? Horehound? Sugar sticks?"

"How much are sugar sticks?" Ruth asked.

"We happen to be having a big sale on sugar sticks today. On account of me being home and all." Amanda opened a small paper sack and took the lid from the sugar-stick jar. "Here's one for David, Zeek, Jeremiah, and Samuel. You three didn't want any of these, did you?"

"Yes, we do, Amanda. We do," Leah said, hardly able to contain the excited whine in her voice.

"Okay then, one each for Ruth, Joseph, and Leah." Amanda put three more of the soft red and white sticks into the sack and added an extra one. "And this one is for Thomas. Will you make sure he gets it?" Immediately after she said that, she regretted her impulsive action. But it was too late, the sugar stick was in the sack.

"We will," the children promised, and took the sack from Amanda.

Joseph said, "Thomas has been gone up on the mountains for a week to cut logs for the sawmill. He just got back a while ago. When he saw that we had our job done, he gave us our penny. He'll like this sugar stick. We'll give it to him right away."

Leah reached up and set the penny on the counter, saying, "We better go now. Mama said, don't be gone too long."

Amanda walked the children out the door and watched them run up the street, carefree, laughing, shouting, and taking turns holding the sack of candy. A part of her wanted to run up the street with them. Closing the door, she went back into the store, her footsteps echoing on the wooden floor. Amanda tightened her apron strings, opened the mail sack, and dumped the contents on the counter. It seemed like a lot of mail for such a small town, but she knew how important it was to a small community on the frontier so far removed from family and friends. Letters and newspapers were their one contact with civilization. Everyone valued the mail like gold. She sorted the magazines and newspapers, then placed them in the proper mailboxes and turned to the letters. One was crumpled and mud-spattered. Its flap was open. It looked as if it had fallen into a water puddle and a horse had stepped on it. But the familiar, ornate handwriting that had haunted her childhood was visible. It was smudged but unmistakable. It was for Thomas, from Elizabeth Avery in Texas. Amanda's hands shook, her stomach knotted. *Is this the way thing are? Still?* She eased open the flap. What would it hurt to take one little peek? Mr. Hunter's words pounded in her head, *The U.S. mail is serious business, Miss Chappell.*

What would one peek hurt?

Serious business . . .

The front door opened. The bell above it tinkled. Amanda jumped, then quickly stuffed the letter into her apron pocket. She took a moment to compose herself, and turned around.

It was him, Thomas Lewellen. Holding his hat in his hand, his dark hair brushed away from his smooth face, he approached the counter smiling, and said, "Hello, Amanda."

He was taller than she remembered, and far more handsome and mature-looking. His dark brown eyes met hers. But she couldn't stand to look for too long. Her knees and voice both shook. "T-T-Thomas."

"It's good to see you again. Welcome to Paradise."

"It's good to . . . to see you, Thomas. It's been a long time."

He smiled and took the sugar stick from his pocket. "I know you gave the children much more than a penny's worth of candy. I'll pay you for the extra."

"That's all right. It was my treat."

He softly laughed, leaned on the counter, and stared at her with his penetrating eyes. "I just had the strangest feeling. This reminds me of the first time I ever saw you. You were sneaking candy out of the horehound jar for you and your friends. I walked in, caught you, and your face turned a bright red, just like now."

Amanda swallowed and tried to laugh. "Th-that's so silly, Thomas. A-um, is there something I can get for you?"

"Just my mail."

"Your mail?" Amanda's face felt hot. She rushed to the mailboxes and grabbed his newspaper. "Here's your paper, I don't have the letters sorted yet. Give me a second to look through them." Amanda turned her back on him and quickly thumbed through the pile of letters, her hands fluttering nervously. She thought, *Slip your*

31

hand in your pocket and sneak the letter back in the pile, no harm done. But another part of her said, *Just one little peek, what would it hurt? One little peek.* Amanda took a deep breath, and protectively placed her hand over her apron pocket. She heeded the latter voice, turned, and said, "I—I'm sorry Thomas, I don't see anything for you right now, maybe next time."

"Thanks, Amanda. I'll see you later." He stuck the sugar stick in the corner of his mouth and walked to the door. At the door he turned, took the candy from his mouth, and said, "Thanks for the sugar stick. It was real sweet of you."

∾∾

Chapter 4

Amanda's cherry-wood desk stood on a raised platform at the front of the room so that when sitting at it, she could see the whole schoolroom. Everything was ready. She was very early, but couldn't help it. First-day-of-school jitters had kept her awake all night. She arose early, fixed her hair, dressed in her new dark blue suit, and arrived at school nervous and anxious. The building was finished. The benches and desks were in place. The room still held the faint smell of the oil they had used to finish the floor. Amanda looked out the tall windows. The morning sun brightened the room. In the back corner, toward the cloak room, stood the ornate wood and coal-burning stove. They wouldn't need it today, but as the term went on, they would. Amanda would be required to arrive early enough, each morning, to set a fire and warm the building before the children arrived.

Amanda opened the narrow, middle drawer of her desk. In the bottom of it sat Thomas's letter from Elizabeth. She had carried it around for several days and hadn't been able to muster the courage to read it, or return it, either. Ever since she had known Thomas, he and the mysterious Elizabeth had exchanged letters.

Back when she and her father were living in the grader's camp and running the store in the tent, her father also had the mail contract and ran a general delivery post office. Every time Amanda sorted the mail for him, she felt a burning hurt each time Thomas received one of Elizabeth's letters from Texas. It hurt worse when he mailed a letter to her.

It seemed funny that Thomas never spoke about her. Usually, when people received mail, they opened it on the spot and shared the news and contents of their letters with anyone who happened to be around in the tent at the moment. But not Thomas; he always politely thanked her for his mail, tucked his letter into his pocket, and took it with him to read at some private moment or place. Amanda could never ask him about it. One of her father's strict postal rules was that you never asked anyone about their mail. If they wanted to tell you about it and share it with you, that was fine. But she was never to ask, and she was always, always to respect the customers' privacy where their mail was concerned. Others in the camp had tried to question Thomas about the letters, saying, "Who's the letter from? Share the news, Thomas. Is that from your lady love?" At most, Thomas gave a half-smile and said, "It's just an old friend."

That seemed like a long time ago, but now, Amanda reached in the drawer, fingered the letter, and felt the familiar pang in her chest, along with a stomach full of guilt. The fact that she had the letter here in her desk drawer went against everything she knew to be right about honesty and respecting others' privacy. It went against her father's rules and against the regulations of the U.S. Postal Service. *Who will know if I take one teeny, tiny little peek?* she thought, and studied the smudged writing. Elizabeth Avery, whoever she was, had beautiful handwriting. It slanted in an elegant, even

34

flow. Amanda took a piece of paper on which she had written the names of her students. By comparison, her own writing seemed merely neat and functional. "Who are you, Elizabeth Avery?" she asked the empty schoolroom, and pictured a genteel southern belle. "I don't even know you, but I hate you. You've made my life miserable since I was twelve years old. I can't stand that you possess Thomas Lewellen's heart, and I never could or will."

Amanda heard a noise on the front steps, tucked the letter into the drawer under her grade ledger, shut it, and went to greet her students. First came the seven Henderson children. They lined their lunch pails, which were a selection of different-sized lard tins with handles, along the wall of the cloakroom. Four-year-old Leah Henderson came, too, and in a proud, self-satisfied voice, said, "I told Mama, I'm coming to school even if I'm not old enough. She said I can come as long as I study hard, keep up with the others, and don't cause trouble."

"That sounds fine to me," Amanda said, and assigned her a seat in the front of the room.

The other children arrived, and by the time school was ready to start, Amanda had assembled all twelve of her students in their desks pretty much by size and age. She sat the smaller children up front, the bigger ones in back. The seven Henderson children made up the majority of her class. There were three Taneman children: Willy, age ten; James, age nine; and Carrie, age six. Their father, Cal Taneman, owned the saloon and the livery barn, the latter which Amanda had been told had a crooked roof. Next were the two McClain children: Marie, age nine, and six-year-old Justin. Their father, Abe McClain, ran the land office and bank.

Amanda spent the morning interviewing and testing each child to find out what grade level he or she was

35

at, so she would know where to start each child's lessons. By the time she was finished, the children seemed restless. "Let's have recess," she told them. The children ran from the building to the open area behind it. Amanda watched them play. One of the Henderson children, eleven-year-old David, had a baseball bat. He stood away from the other children, picking up small pebbles and swinging the bat at them. He was pretty good at hitting the stones a fair distance. Watching him, Amanda felt her own hands itch. It had been a long time since she'd held a bat and swung it at a ball. She walked toward David and said, "That's a nice bat."

"Thank you, Miss Amanda. My pa carved it for me. See?"

He handed the bat to her. Amanda turned it in her hands. The smooth hickory wood had been sanded and oiled. "Where's your baseball?" she asked.

"I had one, but we played with it so much, it just plumb wore out. I never got a new one to replace it. Mama says I have to earn the money myself if I want a new one. Do you still like to play baseball? I remember you used to be good before you went to Omaha."

"To tell the truth, David, this is the first time I've held a bat since the last time you saw me." She gripped the bat and tapped the end of it against the ground. "This has good balance. It's very nice."

"If we had a ball, we could all play, just like we used to."

By now, all of Amanda's students had gathered to watch her look at the bat. "How do you play?" one of the children asked. "Can we play?" another asked.

"We don't have a ball," David said.

"Can we get a ball?" they all seemed to ask together. "Teach us how to play, Miss Amanda. Please? Please?"

"David," Amanda said, "run like a rabbit down to

36

the mercantile, I think I saw a couple of brand-new baseballs under the back counter. Ask Mr. Chappell if he still has them. See if he'll give you one. Have him charge it to me, and bring it back here."

"Yes, ma'am." David ran off at top speed.

"What is baseball?" Carrie asked.

Amanda explained the basics of the game, and said, "Baseball developed from an old English game called rounders. Then during colonial times, in a place called Boston, children just like you played a game using a ball, bat, and one or two bases. They called it *one-o-cat* or *two-o-cat*. As the years went by and the rules changed, the game came to be called *town ball*. It used four bases. Then thirty years ago, in Cooperstown, New York, a man named Abner Doubleday changed the rules a bit more. He called his version of the game *baseball*. His rules are the ones I'll teach you now."

"How did you learn so much about baseball, Miss Amanda?" James asked.

"I love to read. I read everything. Books, magazines, and, especially, newspapers. That's what I hope you will learn to do. When you read, you can learn lots of important and fun things."

David Henderson returned from the mercantile with a brand-new baseball. The children took turns holding the ball while Amanda set a flat rock for home base and paced off a distance to the first base, then second and third, setting a flat rock at each place. "Okay," Amanda said, "we'll divide into teams."

"The girls can't play, can they?" Willy remarked. "I don't want to play with girls."

Amanda said, "Where's the ball?" Zeek passed it to her. She tossed it in the air and caught it. "David, you own the bat. Do you care if our school uses your bat?"

"No, Miss Amanda."

"Good. You see this ball? It belongs to our school.

37

That means it belongs to both the girls and the boys. We all own it equally. Is it fair to say, some can play with it, and some can't because some are girls, or some are too little or too young, or not as athletic as others? Think about it, children. For now, I'm going to take our school baseball into the school building." She walked away.

"Wait, Miss Amanda," Willy called. "I didn't mean it that way. I was just asking."

Amanda faced the children. "Let's get one rule very clear right now. In the Paradise School, we are fair to each other. We don't exclude anyone from anything."

Leah tugged on Amanda's woolen skirt and asked, "What does exclude mean?"

"It means to leave someone out of something, for whatever reason. Like our baseball game, either everyone plays, or no one plays. We don't exclude anyone."

"That's fair," said Marie. "I want to play."

"Does everyone agree?" Amanda asked.

All the children gave her wide-eyed nods. "Come closer," Amanda said. The twelve children gathered close. "We're going to learn many things this year. I'm excited to be the one teaching you. But there is one thing I want you not only to learn, but also to feel. That one thing is this—we have a responsibility to each other. We have to treat each other equally and fairly. We have to respect each other and look after one another. If we do that, we are going to have a wonderful year, and we're going to have fun. But all of us have to live by that rule. Can everyone do that?"

Again, they gave the unison nod.

"Good. Let's play ball."

"Yippee, hooray," the children shouted.

Amanda took David Henderson's bat and tossed the ball to him. "David, let's do a little batting demonstration. Pitch a couple to me. Everyone watch. Especially those of you who haven't ever played before.'' She stood at the flat rock they had set as home base. Taking the bat in hand, she tapped it on the rock, nodded to David, and said, ''Right over the rock, David.''

The ball couldn't have come any more sure and true. Amanda swung the bat and the resounding crack of the bat connecting with the ball echoed as the ball flew up, up, and away toward the road. A horse and rider came down the road, around the trees, right in line with the flying ball. Several things registered in Amanda's brain at the same time. The rider was Thomas. He was going to get hit with the ball. ''Watch out!'' Amanda shouted. ''Look out!'' the children yelled.

Thomas barely had time to look up when the ball smacked him on the side of the head. Amanda and the children ran toward the road. ''Are you all right?'' they asked as he staggered from his horse. Amanda helped him ease off the saddle.

One of the children held his horse while Amanda helped him sit under a tree. She took off his hat and gasped when she saw the red lump rising above his eye. ''Are you all right, Thomas?''

''Wh-what was that?'' Thomas muttered.

''You got hit with a baseball,'' Leah told him.

''A baseball?'' He looked at Amanda. ''Did you hit that ball?''

''Thomas, I'm sorry. I thought we were far enough away from the road. Your eye is going to be so sore.'' She gently fingered the area next to the lump, and her fingers tingled when she touched him. ''Are you all right?''

''Where were you standing when you hit that ball?''

The children all pointed. Two of them, Willy Taneman and Zeek Henderson, ran to home base and stood so he could see where Amanda had been when she'd hit the ball. "My goodness," Thomas exclaimed and scratched his head. "That's a home run if I ever saw one."

"Forgive me, Thomas," Amanda begged.

"On two conditions. First, that you bat away from the road from now on. Second, that you let me play with you for a little while." Thomas got to his feet, led his horse to the tree, tied him, and loosened the saddle cinch.

Amanda divided up the children as evenly as she could by age, size, and what she guessed to be athletic abilities. "Pick your team," she told Thomas when she had the children grouped. "I'll be on the other one. We'll switch home base and second base so we don't bat toward the road any more," Amanda looked at Thomas's puffy eye and winced.

"Good plan," Thomas told her, and smiled. "Roll up your sleeves, Amanda Chappell, I bet you can't hit another one like the last one."

It took a while to fine-tune the rules to allow for the younger children, to make it easier for them to hit the ball and make it to first base. They took time to help the children who had never played baseball before. They gave the girls a second or two to grab their skirts out of the way so they could run to base. Thomas pitched for one team. Amanda pitched for the other. Thomas smacked a couple of home runs. Amanda hit a couple, too.

When the sun stood straight overhead, Amanda looked at her watch and said, "It's almost time to eat. We'd better get our lunches and get back to our studies. Remember, the reason we are here today is school, not baseball."

"Thomas, have lunch with us," the children begged. "I'll share my lunch with you. Me, too. Me, too," they begged.

Thomas agreed and sat in the shade of the cotton-wood tree by the school. Amanda and the children retrieved their lunch pails and sat with him. The children crowded close to him, sitting beside him. "Thanks for visiting our school today," Amanda told him. "I am very sorry about the eye."

Each of the children wanted to share his or her lunch with Thomas. He took small parts of sandwiches from some of the children, and cookies from the rest, until each child had an opportunity to give him something. Amanda was amazed at how the children adored him, just like they had back in the grader's camp—including her.

"Where did you learn to play baseball?" James asked him.

Thomas slowly swallowed the bit of sandwich he was chewing. "I learned when I was a soldier."

"You were a soldier?" Carrie asked, her eyes wide.

"Were you in the big war?" Marie asked.

A pained, far-away look crossed his face. He hesitated before answering. "Yes, I was a soldier in the war between the northern states and the southern states."

"What side did you fight for?" Zeek asked.

"The north. I was a Union soldier."

"Then you were on the winning side," David said.

"It depends on how you look at it," Thomas said, his voice very quiet. "War is a terrible thing. People lose their lives, and property and buildings are destroyed. I try very hard not to think about it."

"How did you play baseball in the war?" Justin asked.

"We did a lot of waiting for orders to tell us where to march next and what to do next. We didn't fight all the time. While we waited for our orders, or in the evenings, some of us teamed up and played baseball. It helped take our minds off the war for a while."

"Did you kill some people?" Carrie asked.

Thomas pulled his watch out of his pocket. "My goodness, look at the time. I've got to go get some nails at the mercantile and get back to work. I shouldn't have stayed away this long. I enjoyed the game very much. Thank you all for sharing your dinner with me. Perhaps you'll let me play with you again sometime." Thomas went to his horse, picked up his hat and put it on, recinched his saddle, mounted, and said, "Thank you for the enjoyable time, Miss Amanda."

"Please, visit our school again," Amanda told him, and watched him ride away, calling, "Take care of that eye."

"Did you know Thomas was in the war?" Ruth Henderson asked.

"I've known Thomas for a long time, but I never knew that about him," Amanda answered.

"Me either," Ruth said.

It makes me think, Thomas Lewellen, Amanda thought as she watched him stop his horse in front of the mercantile, tie it to the hitching post, and go inside. *There's an awful lot about you that I don't know.*

∽∽∾
Chapter 5

During the night, chilly, wet weather moved in, bringing dreary, drippy skies. Dark clouds hung over Paradise, drizzling rain in a heavy mist. Amanda hurried up the muddy street, using an open newspaper as an umbrella. She stomped her feet on the steps of the school, went inside the cold building, and set a fire in the stove. The fire chased away the chill as she swept the floor and dusted the children's desks. While dusting her own desk, she opened the narrow, middle drawer, peeked under the grade ledger at Elizabeth's letter to Thomas, and said to herself, "I've got to get that into his mailbox today. Whatever was I thinking to take it in the first place?" She heard footsteps outside the door and slammed the drawer shut.

The three Taneman children, Willy, James, and Carrie, opened the door and walked into the cloakroom. Amanda went to greet them. "Good morning. How are you this gray morning?"

"Good morning, Miss Amanda," they said.

"Willy, James, could you do me a favor? Take this bucket down to the mercantile and draw some fresh water out of the well for us."

"Sure, Miss Amanda." Willy grabbed the bucket.

Amanda and Carrie stood at the door and watched the two boys run down the muddy street.

Carrie slipped her small hand into Amanda's and said, "It's not very nice outside, is it? Does this mean we won't play baseball today?"

"I'm afraid it does," Amanda answered. "We can't play in the mud. Your mother would be angry with me if I sent you home all muddy."

"What are we going to do, then?"

"We'll think of something. Here come the Henderson children."

Marie and Justin McClain followed soon after the Hendersons. Willy and James Taneman returned with the bucket of water and set it next to the dipper on a bench at the back of the room. Amanda watched the children settle themselves at their desks, and felt like a proud mother hen with all of her little chicks gathered under her wings out of the bad weather. She started the children on their arithmetic. The four oldest children, Willy, David, Marie, and Zeek, helped the younger children, Justin, Joseph, Carrie, and Leah. Amanda helped the middle-age children, Jeremiah, Samuel, James, and Ruth. Later, they switched and the middle graders helped the youngest students while Amanda helped the older children. Then, while the two older groups quietly worked alone on their exercises, Amanda worked with the younger children herself.

After arithmetic, the class took a short break. Some of the children visited the outhouse behind the school. They all got a drink of water, each taking a sip from the dipper by the bucket at the back of the room. Then they returned to their seats to start their reading lessons. When lunchtime came, Amanda said, "Students, put away your readers and get your lunch pails." She looked out the windows. "It's still pretty wet out there. We'll eat inside today."

As they sat at their desks eating, Justin McClain came up to Amanda's desk to show her the cookies he brought. The newspaper that she had used to shield her head that morning was sitting on the corner of her desk. "What's this?" he asked.

"It's a newspaper from Cheyenne. Do you want me to read you something from it?"

All of the children said yes, and after lunch, Amanda seated herself on the edge of the raised platform. The children gathered at her feet, sitting on the floor. She opened the newspaper. It contained a variety of items, including several poems. She read some of them to the children. Then she turned to the front page and had Zeek Henderson read aloud from an article about the upcoming territorial election.

"What's a 'lection?" little Leah asked.

Amanda tried to think of the best way to explain it simply. "We live in the kind of government that is called a democracy. Democracy means rule by the people. In some countries across the ocean, they have kings to rule them. The king makes up the rules and laws. In our country, the people decide what the laws will be. Only think how confusing it would be if everyone in the whole United States had to be a part of every single decision made? It would be very hard because the county is so big. So what we do is vote for a few people to represent us in the decision-making processes of our government. When we vote for a few people who will make our laws and rules, it's called an election. In the upcoming election, we are going to vote for people to represent us in our territorial government."

"What's a territory?" Zeek asked.

"Wyoming is a territory," Amanda answered. "That means we're not an official state in the United States. We want to be a real state someday. Our being a territory is sort of like being on trial or in a test to see if we would make a good state or not. If the United States government decides we would make a good state, it will eventually grant us statehood. Just think, this is Wyoming's very first election. That makes it very special. We'll have to read all about when it happens."

"Are you going to vote in the election?" David asked.

Amanda sighed, "No, I'm not. First of all, I'm not old enough; you have to be twenty-one."

"Wow, that old?" Carrie asked.

"Yes, and I won't be twenty-one for about five more years," Amanda said. "But there's an even bigger problem. I can't vote because women aren't allowed to vote."

"How come?" Zeek asked.

"That's not fair!" Marie exclaimed.

"I know, it doesn't seem fair, does it?" Amanda said, trying to keep her voice calm. "Only men get to vote. Recently, after the big war between the North and the South, the United States government voted to give Negro men the right to vote. So now, all men twenty-one years of age, who are citizens of the United States, have the right to vote, but women don't."

"Is it because women aren't smart enough to vote?" six-year-old Joseph Henderson asked.

"Think about something, Joseph. This morning, Marie seemed smart enough to help you with your arithmetic, didn't she? Could you have done those problems without her help?"

"No, Miss Amanda."

"If she's smart enough to do that, don't you think when she gets older that she'll be smart enough to vote? If I'm smart enough to be your teacher, does that make me smart enough to vote, too? How many think so?" All the children raised their hands. "How many think

46

I should have the right to vote when I'm old enough?'' All the hands went in the air again.

"Why can't women vote?'' Ruth Henderson asked.

"Because we've never been granted that right by the law.''

"Why?'' Marie McClain asked.

"I'm not sure there is a good reason,'' Amanda answered. "We'll have to talk about it another time because it's time to work on our penmanship.'' The children reluctantly returned to their seats. Amanda was pleased with the discussion group that had resulted because of the rain. She decided to have a discussion group every day to talk about current events or whatever the children wanted to talk about.

By the time the school day ended, the rain stopped. The children placed their slates with their penmanship exercises on Amanda's desk. She bid them good-bye, then sat at her desk and studied the slates. Some of the children had good penmanship, others were weak in their lettering. Amanda took a piece of chalk and wrote words of praise or encouragement on the bottom corner of each slate. From down the street, she heard the locomotive whistle blow as the train pulled into the station. She finished her work and took Elizabeth's letter to Thomas from her desk drawer. "Into the mail you go,'' she whispered, tucked it into her pocket, and left the school. Amanda carefully stepped down the muddy street. At one place, she stopped to decide how to best make her way around a puddle, and heard a horse coming from behind her. It was Thomas.

"Hello, Amanda. Wet today, isn't it?'' he said in his deep, smooth voice.

"Wet and dreary.'' Amanda held up her skirts and tried to tiptoe around the edge of the puddle.

He stepped down from his horse and held her elbow to steady her, saying, "No baseball today?''

47

"No baseball or anything outdoors today. The children were very good even though they were cooped up inside all day. The nice thing so far, they all seem to like school very much."

"I liked school when I went. My brothers hated it, though."

Amanda studied him. In all the time she had known him, he had never said anything about his family. "How many brothers do you have?"

A blank, faraway look crossed his face. He took a long time to say, "I have two—two brothers left."

"Left?" Amanda asked, furrowing her brow.

He shook his head. "You don't want to know about this."

Amanda stopped walking, and made him stop. "Yes, I do."

He took off his hat and ran his fingers through his dark hair. "I came from a southern family in east Texas. We owned slaves. My older brother Grayson was a northern sympathizer. You can't imagine the bitter arguments my parents had with him. When the war broke out, my parents disowned him. He took off to go fight with the Union. I believed like he did, and secretly followed after him. When he discovered me, we were too far from home, and it was too dangerous to send me back. I was only eleven years old then. Grayson and I joined the army. He was killed in the battle at Gettysburg." Thomas stopped talking and looked to the sky, studying the clouds and, it seemed, his past, before he continued. "Besides Grayson, I had two other brothers, Chad and Bart, who were southern sympathizers. Then I had two more brothers, Shane and Michael, who were just babies when I left home. Chad and Bart fought in the southern army. They were both killed. I knew they were on the southern side. I can't tell you how awful it was shooting at the other side not knowing, if at any time, I might be shooting at one of my brothers. It left some terrible, terrible memories."

"I'm sorry, Thomas." Amanda had an uncomfortable feeling that she might as well be apologizing to his horse. He seemed not to have heard her, and stood staring into the sky. Down the street, the train sat on the tracks, smoke billowing from the smokestack. The locomotive gave one long whistle, and the train pulled out of the station.

Thomas blinked and his mind seemed to have come back from a faraway place. He said, "Go ahead and go on, Amanda. I'm going to watch the train for a minute."

From where they stood, they could see the train as it slowly pulled out of the station. The cars clipped by as the train picked up speed. There were flat cars, the mail car, boxcars, and livestock cars. Thomas seemed to be silently counting the cars. When the caboose finally rolled by, Amanda said, "You must like trains."

Thomas gave a quiet laugh. "Not really, I got enough of trains when I was building the railroad. I was just counting the cattle cars. There's a man in Omaha who has a huge stockyard. From there, he loads cattle on livestock cars and ships them out here to sell to the army troops at Fort Laramie, Fort Russell, and several other forts. The men in the army eat a lot of beef. I think it's interesting. Think what would happen if the cattle were raised here. You could deliver them to the forts much cheaper without the high railroad-freight costs. This country would make good grazing land . . . Oh, mercy, Amanda. Come on . . . I didn't mean to make you stand out here in the mud while I daydreamed and schemed."

He cupped his hand under her elbow, and they walked side by side. Amanda wanted to hold him and try to comfort him in some way after he had told her

49

about his brothers. But she got the clear feeling he wouldn't talk about them or his family again soon. Not right away. His hand holding her elbow sent a tingle through her body. Her heart tap-danced and pounded in her ears, while at the same time, she remembered the stolen letter in her pocket. Her guilty conscience screamed at her, *This is the perfect time. Give him his letter and apologize. GIVE IT BACK, NOW.*

When they stood in front of the mercantile, Thomas said, "I'm going to check my mail." He tied his horse to the hitching post, and they went into the store. The wet weather had kept several people from their work that day, and they were gathered in front of the potbellied stove, helping themselves to cups of coffee from the enamel pot.

"How was school, Amanda?" asked her father.

"Good."

"Can you sort the mail for me? I haven't had time yet. Everyone is waiting for it."

Amanda donned an apron and opened the mail sack. Jacob and Claire Henderson and Thomas came and stood right where they could watch her. She sorted the magazines and newspapers and put them into the boxes. Then she sorted the letters and flipped them into the proper boxes with quick, efficient movements. When she came to the last letter, she noticed it was addressed to her. "Oh, look, Jacob, do you remember my traveling companion from the train? Laura Barnes?"

"Oh, yes, she was the girl with blonde hair, she was going to a teaching job in . . . ?"

"In South Pass City," said Amanda, slipping her finger under the flap and opening the envelope.

Claire and Thomas both leaned close. The store seemed to go quiet as everyone listened. *"Dear Amanda,"* she read. *"How are you? I had a few minutes and wanted to get a letter written to you. How are*

50

things going at your school? I have seventeen children in my class. They range from ages seven to thirteen. The two oldest boys are thirteen and twelve. They are big for their age, unruly and ornery. I'm at a loss to know what to do with them. They keep my school in a constant turmoil. South Pass City is a rough place that thrives on gold mining. The problem, I think, is that the boys would much rather be out looking for gold. I have the impression, most people here would rather be rich than well-read.''

Cal Taneman, the blonde, bushy-haired owner of the livery barn, laughed and interrupted, "That makes sense to me. Which would you rather have, a bag of gold or a bag of books? Wouldn't take much for me to decide real quick.''

"Shush, Taneman, let her finish the letter,'' Jacob Henderson said, giving Cal a poke in the side with his elbow.

Amanda continued. *"We seem to live from one gold strike to another. The two boys definitely have gold fever and make no bones about the fact that they would rather be out digging in the dirt, looking for gold. It makes them terribly impatient with learning to read and do sums. At the same time, they are so disruptive in class all of the time that it makes it almost impossible to teach anything to the younger children. How are things at your school? I would deeply appreciate any suggestions you might be able to give me.''*

"Tell her to blister their hides good,'' Cal Taneman told her.

"Throw them out of school and be done with them,'' Abe McClain, the banker, said. "It's not fair to the other children to miss out on learning because those two don't want to learn.'' He finished his cup of coffee and said, "I best go close out the bank for the day.'' But he stayed to listen to the rest of the letter.

51

Amanda read more. *"The next bit I'm going to tell you is just gossip I heard, but I think you will be excited to hear it. . . ."* Everyone stepped closer when they heard the word *gossip*. Amanda wished she had a moment to read it by herself before she shared it with the mercantile customers.

"What gossip?" Jacob Henderson asked. "Read it, girl."

"There is a woman . . ." everyone stepped closer, Amanda continued, *"a woman here, named Esther Morris. She is a very tall, older woman, almost mannish in appearance with a rather stern jaw and chin. Her husband owns a saloon here. The talk is, that one afternoon, she held a tea party in her home. Invited to the tea were two men, Colonel William H. Bright and H. G. Nickerson. Both are candidates running against each other for a seat in the legislature in the upcoming election. Mrs. Morris is said to have extracted a promise from them. Both said, that if elected, he will introduce a woman's suffrage bill when he takes office. I don't know if it is true or not, but it is exciting. Just think, Amanda, if that promise is kept, we could be witness to a momentous historical event. I wish I could have been at that tea party. Alas, I am feeling the burdens of being a working woman. When these kinds of momentous events are happening, I am at work, struggling with unruly students who refuse to learn. I've nearly decided, dear Amanda, that the women among us who can truly call themselves liberated are those married to men wealthy enough to afford them housekeepers and nannies so they have time to go to rallies, speeches, and tea parties. They are the women who are free, while I must work to earn a living for myself.*

"But enough of my troubles. Do pray that someone is elected to the legislature who will have the courage and foresight to introduce a bill to grant us the right

to vote. If not, we'll have to declare a war to get it. Take care. Your friend, Laura Barnes.''

"Has your friend taken leave of her senses?" Jacob Henderson thundered. "Women don't need to vote. The law gives them protection and a voice in the government with their husband's vote."

"She doesn't have a husband," Amanda remarked. "Last time I saw her, marriage was the farthest thing from her mind."

Jacob's voice rose, "What kind of a young woman doesn't want a husband so she can share his rights under the law? Tell her to find a husband."

"Give her the vote," Cal Taneman said, his boisterous voice clashing with Jacob's.

"It's blasphemy," Jacob retorted. "I would expect this attitude from someone who can't put a square roof on a building."

No one expected the quick response of Cal Taneman's fist to Jacob's mouth. The smack of his fist against skin made everyone's head pop backward while a stunned silence settled over the mercantile. Jacob sprawled backward against the counter and slid to the floor.

"I'll take my mail," Cal said, smoothing his bushy hair and adjusting his vest.

Her hands shaking, Amanda took the mail from his box and handed it to him.

Taking it under his arm, he said, "I apologize if I offended you ladies in any way. Good day. Jacob Henderson, next time you say Cal Taneman can't put a square roof on a building, you also tell yourself, 'yes, but he can certainly throw a square punch.' " Cal strode out of the mercantile.

Thomas hurried to help Jacob to his feet. A red puffiness surrounded Jacob's mouth. When the shock wore off, Jacob roared, "Did you see that? Did you see

53

what he did?" He ran to the door, stepped out, and yelled, "You goat. I don't have to hope your roof falls in, because I know it will, and I'll be glad when it does."

Claire Henderson stood with her hand over her open mouth. Amanda didn't know what to say. It seemed that no one did. Jacob poked his head in the door and said, "Claire, get the mail." Claire grabbed their mail from Amanda and scurried out the door. Pretty soon, Jacob stomped back in the door and without a word, grabbed his hat off the hat rack, jammed it on his head, and stormed out, banging the door behind him.

"Mercy sakes," Thomas said. "Amanda, next time your friend Laura writes to you, you best not tell a soul. Keep it to yourself, or we'll have a brawl every time the mail train comes. Now, at the risk of starting a battle," Thomas said with a slight snicker, "Can I have my mail, please?"

Amanda reached into his box. He had a newspaper and a catalogue. She remembered his letter from Elizabeth hidden in her pocket and fidgeted as she handed his mail to him.

"Is that all there is?" he asked.

"Seems to be," Amanda said, and thought, *Thomas, if you only knew.*

Chapter 6

The next day came sunny and bright, with only a scattering of clouds, but the baseball diamond was still too wet to play. During noon recess, Amanda and the children sat on the steps in front of the school to eat lunch. Afterwards the boys chased each other in a mad game of tag while the girls took turns braiding Amanda's auburn hair. Amanda closed her eyes and basked in the warm sunshine. Suddenly she heard the shout of angry voices from behind the school. Her eyes flew open and she heard the distinct words, "Fight! Fight!"

Amanda flew from the steps and around the building. The two oldest boys, eleven-year-old David Henderson and ten-year-old Willy Taneman, were locked together rolling in the mud. "Stop it!" Amanda ordered. She pulled the boys apart and to their feet. "What is this about?"

"He called me a name," David Henderson said, swinging a fist at Willy Taneman.

Amanda held David firmly so his fist wouldn't reach Willy's nose. She said, "Willy?"

"He pushed me."

"Did not. It was an accident," David shouted.

"Everyone calm down. Come on." Amanda led them to the front of the building. She sat in the middle of the wide steps, one of the boys on each side of her. "Take a few deep breaths, and in nice, quiet voices, tell me what happened."

Willy said, "We were playing tag, and David was it. He chased me and instead of tagging me, he pushed me real hard on purpose."

David retorted, "I didn't. . . ."

Amanda put her finger to David's lips. "Let him tell his story first, then you'll have your turn."

Willy continued, "I fell down, and look . . ." he pulled up his pant leg. "I hit my knee real hard." There was a nasty, red bruise.

"David?" Amanda said, her voice low and suspicious.

"I was chasing him, but when I reached to tag him, I tripped and fell forward into him. He fell down then, all of a sudden, he jumped up, slugged me and called me a scurvy republican."

"He called you what?" Amanda's mouth dropped open.

"A scurvy republican," David shouted.

Like the ring of a bell, Amanda knew immediately the cause of the underlying tensions behind the fight. "And where did you hear a name like that?" she asked Willy.

Willy worked his mouth back and forth before quietly admitting, "From my pa. He says David's pa, Jacob Henderson, is a scurvy republican. That's why my pa beat the tar outta his pa in the mercantile yesterday."

"He did not," David shouted and reached across Amanda to grab Willy. Amanda nearly had a lap full of wrestling boys before she managed to pull them back into sitting positions.

"Okay, boys. I think we need to talk about this.

Everyone sit. We'll have our current-events discussion for today right here on the steps." The Henderson children sat beside their brother David. The Taneman and McClain children sat on the other side of Amanda beside Willy.

"First of all, who can tell me, what is a scurvy republican?" Amanda studied each of her students. No one offered a hint that they might know. "Do you think we should be calling each other names, when we don't understand what they mean?" With downcast eyes, the children shook their heads. "I was in the mercantile yesterday when Jacob Henderson and Cal Taneman had their disagreement. No one beat the tar out of anyone."

"Didn't somebody hit somebody else?" Marie McClain asked.

"I don't want to talk about the hitting part," Amanda said firmly. "Hitting is wrong, and we aren't going to hit each other in our school. So let's don't talk about who hit whom. The important thing is that two men had a disagreement over something. Is hitting the best way to resolve a disagreement?" All the heads shook in answer. "What's the best way to resolve disagreements?"

"To talk about them," freckle-faced Ruth Henderson suggested.

"You're right. We sit down and talk about them. But what happens if we talk and talk, but we can't agree?"

The children pondered. "Then we fight," eight-year-old Zeek Henderson said, holding his fists up like a boxer.

"No," Amanda said. "What we do is realize that we can't agree. Then we work very hard to understand the other person's point of view. And in turn, we hope they will understand our point of view."

"But that doesn't always work in real life, does it?" Willy Taneman asked, his voice skeptical.

"You're right, Willy. This year we will talk about lots of historical events. I'm very sad to say that history is full of terrible wars and fights, because people couldn't agree on things. They couldn't sit down and respect each other's opinions. Think of the terrible, terrible, terrible war we just got done fighting a few years ago."

"The one Thomas was a soldier in?" Zeek asked.

"Yes, that one, the war between the states. The people in the southern states believed that it was all right to own slaves. The people in the northern states said it was wrong, that no person should own another person. So the states in the south said, fine, we just won't be a part of the United States. We'll start our own country. The states in the north said, oh no you won't, you can't leave. We're one country, and we're going to stay that way. So now the United States had an argument on top of an argument. The two sides bickered until finally, do you know what they did?"

"Did they have a fight?" Leah asked, her eyes wide and questioning.

"They had a terrible, awful fight. Only it was more than a fight, it was a war. Lots of people died and were killed. Whole cities were burned to the ground. Farms and businesses were destroyed. It will be a very long time before everything that was damaged is fixed or rebuilt, and it will cost so much money, you can't even begin to understand how much money."

"Like how much money?" Zeek Henderson asked.

"Like if you had a flour barrel full to the top with money, it still wouldn't be enough."

Marie McClain said, "My father said that a whole bunch of people died in that war."

"That's right," Amanda said, remembering what she'd read about the battle at Gettysburg, where Thomas's brother died. In that one, single battle of the war, 61,000 soldiers were killed, wounded, or missing.

Amanda couldn't begin to try to explain that fact to the children. She didn't know how to help them understand how big the number was, and didn't know herself how to understand the magnitude of that many destroyed and ruined human lives.

Little Leah climbed into her lap. "I don't like war," she said, burying her face into Amanda's shoulder.

"I don't either, sweetie," Amanda said, holding her and noticing that all the children seemed to have snuggled a little closer to her. "That's why we need to learn to talk about our differences and try to work them out before they cause a fight. Even though it isn't easy, we need to learn to respect each other's differences starting right here in our own little school. David and Willy, your fathers disagree on something. We can't change that. But what we can do is not bring those differences to school with us. Yesterday, you two were good friends and today, you're fighting. What are we going to do about that? Any suggestions?"

The children pondered for a moment, then most of them shrugged.

"What do you say to this idea? See the road running in front of the school? When we come to school and cross that road, let's leave our parents' disagreements and their worries that have nothing to do with our school on the other side of the road. The differences we have, that have to do with our school, we'll promise to work them out between ourselves. What do you say?"

"That's a good idea," said Zeek Henderson.

"Willy, David? What do you say?"

"That's good," said David. "I'm sorry if I hurt you, Willy. I didn't mean to push you. I tripped and fell forward and accidentally pushed you."

Willy stretched his hand across Amanda's lap and

59

offered his hand to David. "I'm sorry too," he said. "Shake?"

Amanda held their joined hands in her own. "I'm very proud of you, and I'm proud that we have the best school in Wyoming Territory. What does everyone say? If you agree, put your hands here in a group, and we'll all shake. Are we going to leave our parents' disagreements and problems on the other side of the street?"

Each of the children put a hand on top of Amanda's hand in a communal handshake. "Very good," said Amanda.

"But what is a scurvy republican?" Zeek asked.

"Let me see if I can explain that one. Scurvy is a disease where you get very sick and weak and your teeth fall out."

"Yuck," said Willy.

"What a republican is, is a little harder to explain. When we have elections in this country there are two main parties, the republicans and the democrats."

"Do the parties have cake and pie?" Leah asked.

"Oh, boy," said Amanda. "It's not a party like a birthday party. It's a party like a group of people. There is a group of people called the Democratic Party and a group called the Republican Party."

"What's the difference?" David asked.

"The difference in the people in the parties is in how they want the government to work and to run. Think of it like this: we have one school. Think of the whole United States as being like our school. But then, our school is divided into two baseball teams that play baseball against each other. That's how the democrats and republicans are. They play politics against each other, each trying to win the elections and the votes on the ideas they want to make into laws for us. Sometimes they get into big arguments over some of their ideas. When you grow up, you can decide if you want to be a democrat or a republican, and chose which party you want to join.''

"Are you a democrat or republican?'' Willy asked.

"Seeing how I don't get to vote, it doesn't make sense for me to choose, does it?''

"How come you can't vote?'' Ruth asked.

"Remember how we talked about that yesterday? I can't vote because I'm a girl. If the government ever changes that law, I'll be able to vote. Then I'll decide which team, I mean, which party, I want to be a member of.''

"That's not fair,'' Ruth said. "You should vote because you know an awful lot about elections and things.''

"Do you know why I know lots of things?''

"Because you love to read a lot,'' the children shouted in unison.

"That's right,'' Amanda told them, surprised that they remembered what she'd told them earlier. "If you read a lot, you'll know a lot, too. And maybe someday they'll pass a law so that I can vote. I hope they do. It's very important to me.''

"Why?'' David asked.

"Because when you vote, it is your way of having a voice in the government. Our voices are heard when we cast ballots and vote in elections. I would very much like to have a voice in the process that makes the laws by which I am ruled. When you boys get old enough, you'll be able to vote. Don't ever forget what a special right, and privilege, that is.''

"We should name our baseball teams the Republicans and the Democrats,'' Zeek suggested.

"I don't know,'' Amanda said hesitantly. "In real life, the republicans and democrats fight too much, and they don't get along very well sometimes. Our two teams get along better than that.''

61

"What will we call our teams, then?" Ruth asked.

"Let me see," said Amanda. "If you know much about baseball, way back, about twenty-three years ago, one of the first recorded, organized baseball games was played between two teams called the New York Knickerbockers and the New York Nine. The Knickerbockers lost to the Nine. We could have our teams named in honor of them. We'd have the Paradise Knickerbockers and the Paradise Nine."

"But we only have six people on each team not counting you, Miss Amanda," Willy observed. "You pitch for both teams, unless Thomas happens to play with us."

"We could be the Paradise Knickerbockers and the Paradise Six," said Ruth Henderson.

"Wait a minute," said Amanda. "Let's be democratic about this, take a vote."

"Do only the boys get to vote?" Carrie asked with a whine in her voice.

"Nope," said Amanda. "In our democratic school, everyone has a voice because everyone has a vote. Both girls and boys vote. We're voting for whether to call one of the teams the Nine or the Six. Raise your hand if you want it to be the Paradise Nine." Five hands went in the air. "How many for the Paradise Six?" Seven hands shot in the air. "Paradise Six wins by two votes. Should we call the other team the Knickerbockers? Raise your hand if you think so." All the hands went in the air. "The Paradise Knickerbockers it is."

"Which team gets which name?" David asked.

"Tell you what," said Amanda, "we could have a game to decide. The winning team gets to choose which name they want. You know what else we could do? We could invite our parents to come watch."

"Can we have a picnic, too?" Marie asked.

"That's a great idea, Marie. Does everyone want to do that?"

"Let's do," the children agreed, the excitement showing in their faces.

"Everyone who wants to do that, raise your hand." All the hands went in the air. "We'll plan on it. Now, we'd better go in and finish up our work. Copy your penmanship exercises on your slates and put them on my desk. Then we'll call it a day."

When the slates were piled on Amanda's desk, the children seemed reluctant to go home to their chores. They were too excited about the game and picnic. Amanda walked them to the road and bid them goodbye. As she turned to go back to the school, she heard her name being called.

Thomas, on his sorrel horse, trotted up beside her. "Hello, Amanda. I figured it was still too wet for baseball today."

"It was. But we're planning a very important game and picnic. The winner of the game gets to choose one of two names we're going to name our teams."

"What names?"

"The Paradise Knickerbockers and the Paradise Six."

"Can I play?"

"It'll be up to the children."

"How can they refuse me, Amanda? I'll see you tomorrow. I have an appointment to get my horse shod, and I'm a bit late. I'll talk to you later." He turned his horse and trotted off toward the livery barn.

Amanda's pulse thumped in her temples as she thought, *How could they refuse you, indeed, Thomas Lewellen. How well I know. I've been trying to tell my heart to refuse you for four years now. A lot of good it's done me.*

Amanda went into the school and took her shawl

from the back of the chair. Then she opened the middle desk drawer, groaned, took Elizabeth's letter from under the grade ledger, and slipped it into her pocket. That morning she had put it in her desk drawer again after she had failed to give it to Thomas the day before. She thought about the letter and told herself, *Thomas, you've turned me into a crazy, stealing woman. I should hate you for making me feel like a childish, unworthy fool.* "I do hate you, Thomas," she told the empty schoolroom. "Sort of," she added, and left the building.

Chapter 7

That evening, Amanda sat at the mercantile counter on a high stool. The oil lamp cast a warm glow on her sign. It said WE NOW HAVE FRESH EGGS in large block letters. The sign was for her father. Mrs. McClain's hens were laying more eggs than her family could use, and William was going to sell them in the mercantile.

While Amanda waited for the ink to dry, she took another sheet of paper to write a letter to Laura Barnes. Amanda told her how sorry she was about the unruly boys in her class and that she hoped things were going much better for her by now. Then she wrote:

> My class is just wonderful. I have twelve students. I was excited to hear about the tea party, and the candidates' promises. Did it really happen? Will the future legislator from South Pass City actually introduce a bill for women's suffrage? Can you imagine it, Laura? If they pass the law, women in Wyoming Territory will be the first women in the entire world ever to vote in a general election. I'm so excited about the progress. Please write to me if you hear more about

it. I read your letter to some of the people who were in the mercantile. I'm afraid there isn't much privacy here. The mail comes in three times a week. When it does, people seem to gather in the store, then read their letters to everyone else. We are so hungry for news of things happening every-where else that we don't care who the letters are from, just that they bring fresh news. When I shared your letter, especially the part about wom-en's suffrage, it caused a heated exchange of words between two of our citizens. The argument ended when one of them slugged the other in the mouth. The next day, it led to a fight between two of my students, who were the children of the two men involved in the altercation. The children worked it out and are best friends again. I hope the two adults will work out their differences as well as the children did. I best go for now. I have a few more things to do before I'm off to bed. Good night, dear Laura. With love, your friend, Amanda.

Amanda pulled an envelope from the drawer, ad-dressed it, and popped in the letter. She took it to the post office counter, applied a stamp from the drawer, and canceled it with the rubber stamp that said *Para-dise, Wyoming Territory*. Into the outgoing mailbox it went. Amanda checked her sign. The ink wasn't quite dry yet. She felt her pocket. Thomas's letter was tucked inside. Going to the bottom of the stairs, she listened for her father, who was relaxing in the sitting room, the pages of a newspaper rustling as he turned them. Amanda pulled the stolen letter from her pocket. *I've held on to this far too long,* she told herself, turning the envelope over in her hand and lifting the flap. "To-morrow, when the mail comes, to your rightful owner you're going. But then again . . . you're already open . . . who would know if I took one little peek?" She slightly opened the envelope and tried to read the smeared words. Unable to read it, she sat on her stool, pulled the oil lamp closer, and tried to see through the heavy paper. Amanda closed her eyes and eased the letter part of the way out of the envelope. "Just a little more." Soon, bit by bit, the letter was all but out of the envelope. "I have it this far," she whispered. "I've already done a bad thing, I might as well do a real bad thing and read a little bit of it."

Her father's footsteps sounded overhead. She jumped from the stool and went to the bottom of the stairs again, to listen.

"Amanda," he called.

"Yes, father?" She tried to keep her nervousness out of her voice.

"I think I'm going to say good night. Are you all right? That sign seems to be taking a long time."

"I finished the sign. It's drying. I'm writing a letter to Laura. I want it to go out tomorrow."

"Good night, then, sweetheart."

"Good night, Father." She heard muffled footsteps moving toward his bedroom. Amanda returned to the stool, picked up the letter, and unfolded it. Most of the first page was smeared until it was illegible. She turned the page, and made out the words, *I hope you will understand. I'm engaged to be married. We can still write and continue our secret relationship. . . .* Amanda could not make out the next section of words. *I won't be able to write much while the wedding preparations are in progress . . . but after I'm married I can make arrangements so we can keep writing. I will try to sneak a letter off to you whenever I can. It will be best if you don't write to me for a while. I will tell you when it is safe and will send you an address where you can reach me. I'm willing if you are. Dear Thomas, I love you so, and I'm sorry things have to be this way . . . I wish they were different. All my love . . . Your Elizabeth.*

Amanda refolded the letter and put it in the envelope. A sick feeling nagged at her stomach. *What kind of person is this?* she wondered. *What kind of shameless woman would write about getting married and at the same time ask another man to keep sending her letters?* Amanda dropped the letter on the countertop, not wanting to touch it again, it made her so uncomfortable. *How would Thomas react? Would he agree to such an arrangement? If he did agree, what kind of person did that make him?* "Thomas," she whispered to the shelves full of tins and boxes, "how little I actually know about you. Is it possible that you don't see how much I care about you, no matter how much I've tried not to? That's what hurts me the most. You don't seem to see." She wiped a tear from her cheek. The ink on her sign was dry, so she tacked it on the shelf behind the cash register, then gathered her pens and started to put the cork in the bottle of ink. Her hand paused. She set the cork on the counter, took another piece of paper and a pen in hand. Pulling her letter out of the envelope again, she studied the handwriting. "What do you have, Elizabeth Avery, that I don't have?" Amanda dipped the pen in the ink and wrote her name on the paper. Her handwriting was so ordinary, Elizabeth's so elegant. She copied part of the letter, trying to get her writing to look like Elizabeth's, and got frustrated when it didn't match perfectly. After several tries, her lettering was getting close to looking like Elizabeth's. She took a piece of stationery from the drawer and poised the pen above it.

Dear Thomas, she slowly and carefully wrote, emulating Elizabeth's handwriting. *I have loved you since I was a little girl. What do I have to do to show you?*

How do I find the courage to say, please love me, please marry me? With love, Amanda paused, unable to sign her own name. "This is the letter you should have written," she said to the invisible Elizabeth Avery in her mind. "Or something like it." She carefully signed the word *Elizabeth* at the bottom of the page. Taking another envelope, she addressed it to Thomas, put her letter into it, took it back to the postal counter, and applied a stamp. Amanda pressed the cancellation stamp on the envelope and slightly twisted it so the cancellation would be smudged and illegible.

"There," she said and studied her work. She couldn't read the words, *Paradise, Wyoming Territory* at all. "No one would know," she whispered, "where this came from." She tapped the envelope on the counter, sighed, and told the envelope, "Now that I've had my little bit of fantasy and fun, into the stove you go. Your fate, like that of my feelings for Thomas, is to be ashes." Amanda returned to her pens and ink, set her own letter on top of Elizabeth's, put the cork in the ink bottle, gathered the pens together, and put them and the ink into their proper places in the drawer. Amanda heard a footfall on the steps. Her father was coming down the stairs. She stuffed the letters into her pocket, grabbed the dust rag, and wiped the counter where she had been working.

"Still at it?" her father asked, coming through the curtains wearing his nightshirt and robe.

"All finished," Amanda said. "I was just about to come up to bed. I thought you had gone already."

"I had, but I have a bit of a stomachache, so I came down for something to settle it." He took a tin of Glauber's Bicarb Pills from the shelf. He eyed the sign Amanda had hung earlier. "That looks real nice. Thank-you. When it comes to making signs, I'm afraid I'm not as neat as you are."

69

"Thanks, Father. Anytime you need one, just ask."

"I will." He put his arm around her. "Amanda, I don't think I've told you since you've been home how glad I am that you are here. I missed you terribly when you were in Omaha. Now you are so grown-up and such a fine teacher. I'm very proud of you."

Amanda gave him a hug. "I'm glad to be here, too, Father. I don't ever want to be away from you again."

He laughed. "Someday soon, I expect someone will ride into town and steal both your heart and you away from me."

"I don't think that is ever going to happen."

"I fully expect it will, but it won't be tonight, and I have freight coming tomorrow. Let's not worry about it for now and get some sleep."

Amanda blew out the lamps. Her father held a lit candle as they made their way up the stairs. He gave her one last hug and said, "Good night."

In her bedroom, Amanda undressed and hung up her woolen skirt, knowing she would be wearing it again the next day. After she washed up, brushed her hair, and dressed in a nightgown, she blew out the lamp and crawled into bed. A little voice inside her head reminded her to go throw her imitation of Elizabeth's writing into the stove. Amanda curled into a comfortable ball under the quilt. "I'll get it tomorrow," she told the little voice, then fell asleep.

The next morning, Amanda dressed for school, patted her skirt pocket where the letters were tucked, and promised herself she would burn her letter and return Elizabeth's letter to Thomas's mailbox.

Amanda left the store and headed for the school. When she got there, Willy Taneman was sitting on the steps. His eyes were swollen and red. "Willy, whatever on earth is the matter?"

Willy sniffed and said, "This morning, Jacob Henderson told me his children weren't ever coming back to school again. He told me to tell you as much.''

Amanda felt like a huge fist had rammed into her gut. "What?'' She sunk down on the steps next to Willy. "Why?''

"I don't know. David and I were going to come to school early this morning so we could practice batting. David wasn't here when I got here, so I walked up the road to meet him. I got all the way to his house and knocked on the door. Jacob Henderson answered. He said for me to get off his porch and go home, 'cause he didn't want any relation of Cal Taneman's in his house. He said his children were not going to go to a school where the teacher pollutes their minds with suffrage junk and talk about women voting.''

Amanda's eyes filled with tears. "I haven't polluted anyone's mind.''

"Can he do this?'' Willy asked.

"I don't know,'' Amanda whispered. "We'll have to see.'' She knew that if Jacob Henderson didn't want to send his children to school, there was nothing in the world anyone could do to make him. She put her arm around Willy and said, "It'll be all right. Wait and see. We'll work it out. David and the rest will be back before we know it.'' She gave him a reassuring smile, and the other students, except for the Hendersons, arrived.

The morning passed slowly. A pervasive sadness permeated the schoolroom. Amanda tried to keep a smile on her face and kept telling the children that their friends and classmates would be back soon. None of the children had any enthusiasm for lessons. Even though Amanda worked to keep her voice cheery and bright, she couldn't help feeling like a gloomy shadow followed her every step all morning.

By noon, the Henderson children still hadn't come to school. Amanda and the other children sat on the schoolhouse steps, eating their lunches and saying very little. They watched Thomas walk up the road. Amanda told the children to wait on the steps. She ran toward him. "Thomas, have you talked to Jacob? He can't mean to keep his children out of school, can he?"

He took off his hat. "Amanda, I'm sorry. Jacob can be pretty stubborn sometimes. He sounds positive his children will never return."

Amanda's eyes filled with tears. "I don't understand. I never polluted their minds. We had discussions and talked about controversial things. But I told the children they have to make up their own minds about the things we talk about. He has to let his children come to school." A tear slipped from her eye and down her cheek.

Thomas slid his arm around her. "It'll be all right," he whispered, "you'll see."

Amanda couldn't help herself, she started to cry. "I never thought Jacob would do something like this to me or to his children. How could he? Doesn't he care about their education, or about our school? We need his children to have a better school."

Her tears fell on the soft fabric of his cotton shirt. Amanda allowed herself to be comforted by him, until she realized that she was in his arms and the rest of her students were watching. She quickly pulled away, her mind a confused whirl of thoughts. Wiping her eyes, she said, "I imagine you'll want to take David his bat. We don't have enough children to play baseball any more. I better send the bat with you. No, wait. If I take it, maybe I can talk to Jacob."

"Good luck," Thomas said, "I'm sorry about the baseball game today. I was looking forward to booting one of your pitches over the treetops." Amanda half smiled. "Here comes that pretty smile of yours," he said, and reached out gently to wipe the last tear from her cheek. "Don't worry, pretty Amanda, sometimes these kinds of things take time. Be patient. Jacob will come around, eventually."

Amanda felt the burning trail that his finger left on her face. While one part of her welcomed his touch, the other part of her silently screamed, *Don't do that. Don't touch me. I can't stand it if you touch me like that when I know you don't love me.*

Chapter 8

After school that day, Amanda hurried toward the mercantile carrying the baseball bat. At the mercantile, she set the bat in a corner and donned an apron. Her father was out, behind the store, unloading crates from the wagon and carrying them upstairs to the storeroom. "I haven't had time to go get the mail, yet," he told her, tugging on a heavy crate.

"I'll take care of it," Amanda said, grabbing the outgoing mail sack and rushing to the train station. Mr. Hunter, the stationmaster, was talking to the uniformed train conductor on the wooden platform. Amanda stepped up on the platform and handed the mail sack to Mr. Hunter. He gave it to the conductor, who waved to the engineer in the locomotive. Tipping his hat to Amanda, he said good-bye to Mr. Hunter and stepped aboard the train with the mail sack. The whistle blew, and the wheels moved with a squeal of metal against metal as the train pulled away from the station. Amanda followed Mr. Hunter into the station house. He hesitated before handing her the incoming mail sack. "The Cheyenne Leader newspaper that everyone subscribes to didn't make the train today. It'll come next time. Here are some sample copies of a new paper." He handed her a bundle. "It's the Cheyenne Eagle. I imagine they want people to subscribe, so they sent us some free copies."

"Thank you, Mr. Hunter. I'll see that every family gets one."

He held the papers, not willing to give them to her that easy. His mustache bobbed as he nervously worked his mouth, trying to find the right words to ask a question. Amanda waited patiently, then prompted, "Do you want to ask me something, Mr. Hunter?"

"Well . . . I don't know . . . it isn't such a big deal . . ."

Amanda got an uncomfortable feeling. "What is it, Mr. Hunter?"

"Well . . ." Finally, his voice exploded into a rush of words, "I just don't know why the mail has to be such a big deal around here."

Amanda remembered the time she was late getting the mail to the station. His rough words had told her to remember that the U.S. mail was serious business. She felt a twinge of guilt when she thought about the letters hidden in her pocket. *What changed his mind?* she wondered, and asked, "What do you mean?"

"Everyone makes such a big deal of the mail all the time. I don't know why it has to be such a big fuss, everyone gathering at the store to read their letters aloud, like as if it was any one else's business what mail they get. It's just plain silliness."

Amanda had a hint of an idea about what he was getting at. "Mr. Hunter, do you want to mail a letter to someone, or are you expecting a letter, that you don't want everyone else to know about?" The skin around his mustache turned a bright red. "I know the U.S. mail is serious business," she said. "But we are allowed to make some exceptions. What if you have a letter you want to mail so you just give it to me? I'll carry it up to the mercantile, put a stamp on it, cancel it, then slip it in the outgoing mailbox. No one but me will know about it, and I'm not allowed to tell. If you get a letter, I'll quietly set it aside and bring it down here. You won't have to come into the store to get it.''

"You could do that?''

"I could, and I wouldn't tell. ''

"Well, fine.'' He slapped an envelope and a nickel on the counter. "Keep the change,'' he barked in a gruff voice. "Get yourself a sugar stick or something.'' He turned his back and shuffled the papers on his desk.

Amanda picked up the letter and the nickel. "Good-day, Mr. Hunter.'' He gave a sharp grunt, and the telegraph key started its vibrating, clicking tune. He turned his attention to it. Amanda tucked the letter into her pocket beside Thomas's letter from Elizabeth and her forged imitation letter. When she left the station house, she saw Thomas, sitting on his sorrel horse watching the train rolling out of the station. "Still dreaming about cattle?'' she asked.

"Hello, Amanda.'' Thomas turned from the train as the caboose rolled by and the noise of the train disappeared. He climbed down from the saddle and walked up the street beside her, leading the horse. "Every time I see a train, I wonder about all the possibilities,'' he said with a smile. "I better get my mail and go home. I'm going to work on my house tonight.''

"I hear it's very nice.''

"I like it. You'll have to come up and see it. The outside is done, but I have a lot to do on the interior.''

"I'll come see it sometime,'' she told him as they reached the door of the mercantile.

Amanda hurried to go inside the store. He wrapped the horse's reins around the hitching post, and stepped behind her to hold the door for her. He was so fast, she couldn't slip into the store before he did. He seemed to be on her heels all the way into the store, which was full of people waiting for their mail. The Taneman family and the McClain family were there. The children gathered around Amanda, asking questions and wrapping their arms around her. "Hello, Miss Amanda. What are we doing in school tomorrow? Are the Hendersons coming back to school tomorrow?"

A cold sweat crept up Amanda's neck. *How am I going to slip Thomas's letter into the mail with all of these people and this hubbub going on around me?* As she donned her apron, she slipped her hand into her pocket and grabbed Mr. Hunter's letter. In an easy movement, she slipped it into the outgoing mailbox. "What's that?" Willy Taneman asked as he leaned over the counter, watching her.

"Just outgoing mail," Amanda answered and dumped the contents of the sack onto the back counter. She could feel everyone's eyes burning into her backside as she sorted the magazines and catalogues from the letters. "The Cheyenne Leader didn't make the train, so we didn't get it, but there's a new paper in Cheyenne. They sent us some sample copies. It's called the Eagle. There are enough copies for everyone." She slipped a newspaper into each box. They were all watching her.

When she turned from the boxes, she felt in her pocket, touched the loose flap on Elizabeth's letter, and mentally chastised herself. *Why didn't I throw my silly fake letter into the stove at school when I had the opportunity today?*

Thomas leaned on the counter. "Anything for me today?" he asked.

"We'll know in a minute," Amanda said, trying not to sound nervous. She turned partway around, looked up at the plate glass windows, and pointed. "Look," she said. In the split second that everyone looked, she pulled an envelope from her pocket and buried it in the pile of letters.

"What did you see? What was it?" everyone asked.

"I thought I saw someone ride by, but I was wrong. It must have been my imagination. I'm sorry. Let me get these letters sorted so you can have your mail. Let's see, we have one for Taneman, for Taneman, for McClain, for the mercantile, for . . ."

"For who?" Willy Taneman asked.

"For . . . for . . . for Thomas." As Amanda held the letter, horror filled her chest. It was the wrong letter. It was her forged letter, not Elizabeth's real letter. Amanda couldn't breathe. *What have I done,* she thought, not knowing what to do next. "I can just slip it into your box, Thomas, and give it to you . . . when . . . when . . . when I see if you have more letters." Amanda's hands shook, her stomach lurched, and she thought she might vomit.

"There won't be more," Thomas said. "I'll just take it and my newspaper and be on my way."

"Thomas, wouldn't you like to have some coffee? Maybe you need to do some shopping before you're ready to go," she suggested. Her skin felt like it was crawling over her bones.

"No, I just need my mail." He held out his hand for his letter.

Amanda held it protectively against her apron. The room went quiet. "Thomas . . ." she whispered.

"Are you all right?" Mrs. McClain asked. "Your cheeks look so pale."

"I'm fine," Amanda said, slowly reaching to hand him the letter. "Thomas, perhaps you don't really want to read this . . ."

"Quit teasing, Amanda. Of course I want to read it." He took the envelope from her and tucked it into his shirt pocket. "I'll read it when I eat my supper."

"Aren't you going to read it now? Come on, Thomas, share it. Don't be stingy, read it to us," everyone begged.

"I'll see you all later," he said in his light southern drawl, then put on his hat, tipped it, and left.

Amanda's knees went weak. She closed her eyes and held her breath. *Whatever have I done now,* she thought, misery engulfing her.

That night at supper, Amanda picked at her stew. Her tongue felt flat and lifeless.

"What's the matter?" her father asked.

"Nothing," she said, and mechanically stirred her food.

"Jacob Henderson came in today."

Amanda looked at her father. "Did he tell you about the children?"

"Yes. I'm sorry, Amanda. He also made me declare where I stood on the women's suffrage issue. I told him I was for it, because I think there are many women like you out in the world with your intelligence and education who read about and care about the issues. You should vote just like me or any other man."

"Father, thank you for that. Thank you for standing up for me."

"I wasn't standing up for you; it's what I believe."

"What did Jacob say to that?"

"His face turned red. He shouted some angry words and said he would never shop in the mercantile again. He and some of the other families who live out of town have sworn not to shop in here again. Jacob said he had secured their promises that, unless I change my mind, they won't shop here."

"Father, we can't let this scrape I've gotten us into hurt your business."

"We've weathered storms before; we'll weather this one."

"I shouldn't have talked about any of those things at school. I didn't tell the children to believe what I believe. I told them they have to decide for themselves how they feel about the things we discuss. What's wrong with having a discussion about the issues facing us today? I never said one side is wrong and one is right. How does that pollute a child's mind? The children were interested. If they had been interested in knitting or lizards, we would have discussed knitting or lizards. I'm very worried about this and how it will hurt the store."

"Amanda, you don't have to explain it to me. I understand. Don't worry about the store. Jacob and some of the others will go to Cheyenne to shop for a while, then they'll get tired of traveling so far for groceries and supplies. Or they may order their supplies and groceries from the catalogue. They'll get tired of backstocked items, items that don't come, and orders that don't get put on the train when they're supposed to. Eventually, they'll swallow their pride and come back to shop, at first for a few necessary items, then for a few items more. Then, all of a sudden, I'll be filling all of their orders again. It just takes time. Besides, they have to come here to get their mail, so I don't think their indignation, or their ill feelings, will last too long. They'll want their mail sooner or later." He reached across the table and patted Amanda's hand. "If you're not going to eat that stew, let's put up the dishes and get some sleep. I'm tired after unloading all that freight today and digging in the root cellar. Don't worry. It'll be all right."

They washed the dishes. William chatted about the weather and the freight that had come. Amanda was very quiet. When they set the last dish on the shelf, they dumped the dirty dishwater in the slop bucket and bid each other good night.

In her bedroom, Amanda undressed, blew out the lamp, crawled under the quilts, and stared up at the ceiling. Tears filled her eyes and plopped on the pillow. It had been a strange, horrible day. She mourned the loss of half of her students because of her personal political beliefs, which had also caused the loss of some of her father's customers. Thinking about the mix-up of letters made her cheeks burn. "What have I done?" she whispered. "Surely Thomas has read my forged letter. What did he think?"

She remembered when he had stopped by the school earlier that afternoon. Once again, Amanda felt his arms around her and the tingling touch of his finger on her cheek. She felt the tingling sensation again as clear and strong as it had been then. Wiping at her cheek, Amanda willed the tingling feeling to go away, but it grew and spread down her neck, into her stomach, down her legs, to the tips of her toes. She climbed out of bed and poured water from the pitcher into the basin. She scrubbed and scrubbed at her face with the cool water, trying to make the feeling quit. It refused to go away. She buried her face in a towel and let her mouth open while she silently screamed into its rough depths. *Thomas,* she thought. *Why didn't you get on your horse and go back to Texas when the railroad was finished? Why do you have to be here in Paradise, so that I have to see you and remember that no matter how hard I try, I will always love you?*

She looked out of the window and whispered to the stars twinkling above. "What do I have to do to get him out of my system? I'm doing crazy, irrational, stupid, dishonest things because of him. Oh, that I had never taken his letter in the first place, that I had

81

never played with fate, or been so nosy. How do I undo what I've done? Tell me, little stars, what should I do now?''

The stars only winked, blinked, and offered no answers or comfort.

Chapter 9

After school the next day, Amanda went to the mercantile and donned an apron. As she tightened the strings around her waist, she noticed David Henderson's bat standing in the corner, and had an idea. She pulled the Henderson mail out of its box and rolled the catalogue and newspaper together. Taking the bat and the mail, Amanda told her father she was stepping out for a minute, and left the store.

The late afternoon sun warmed her back as she walked toward the Henderson house. When she arrived, the seven Henderson children poured out of the house, hugged her, and said, "Amanda! Amanda, we're glad to see you." She gave David his bat. He thanked her with a smile and eyes full of sadness.

Their father, Jacob, stepped out of the house and loudly cleared his throat. The children quickly backed away and lowered their heads. "You have chores, don't you?" he said, his voice gruff. They scurried into the house. "What do you want?" he demanded.

Amanda said, "Jacob, if I've done something to make you angry, I'm terribly sorry. Don't punish the children for something I've done. Please, let them come to school."

"My children will do just fine right here at home. Claire will teach them what they need to know without all that women's voting garbage."

"We won't talk about it in school again. I promise." Amanda felt tears of anger well up in her eyes. She blinked them away.

"What about your pa? I won't do business with someone who thinks like he does. I am the head of my house. I will vote for my family's best interests and take care of them. Me. I do that. Your pa would do well to do the same."

"Jacob, think about the years we were together in the grader's camp. You and Claire are like family to me and my father. Can't we forget all this and remember that before our disagreements, we are family. I brought David's bat, and here's your mail. There wasn't much, just a catalogue and the paper."

Jacob looked at the masthead and said, "Ah, the Leader. I'll read it tonight."

"It's not the Leader. It's a free sample of a new paper. The Leader didn't get put on the train; it'll come on the next train."

Jacob's voice filled with defensive bitterness, "I can see that for myself. Now get out of here. We don't need your women's suffrage talk around here." He stomped into the house, slamming the door behind him.

Turning on her heel, Amanda walked away, her head full of confusion. One minute, they seemed to be having a reasonable conversation. The next minute, she was being sent down the road like a whipped puppy with its tail between its legs. She wondered, *How did he get to be so stubborn and hardheaded?*

Two days later, Amanda prepared the outgoing mail. She sorted through the envelopes, making sure all the stamps were canceled. As she thumbed through the envelopes, she stopped at the stationmaster's letter. It was addressed to the *Des Moines, Iowa, Lonely Hearts Society.* Amanda smiled and understood why Mr. Hunter was so particular about who did and didn't see his mail. Heaven knew what a stir and teasing it would cause if everyone knew he was looking for a sweetheart. She dropped his letter into the mail sack, whispering, "Cupid speed your way, little letter. Maybe you'll bring Mr. Hunter better luck in love than I've had."

"Hello, Amanda."

She spun around at the sound of the deep, familiar voice. "Thomas, hello, I didn't hear you come in, did the bell above the door ring?"

"Yes. I guess you were so involved with what you were doing, you didn't hear it."

"I'm getting the mail ready to go out tomorrow."

"Here's another letter for your sack." He laid an envelope on the counter. "And I need a can of saddle soap, a little coffee, and a couple of those sugar sticks."

Amanda gathered the items together and totaled up his ticket. "Do you want this on account?"

"Yes, please." He picked up the sugar sticks. She wrapped the other items in brown paper and tied them with a string.

"Here you are, Thomas. Thank you."

He put the package under his arm, tasted a sugar stick, and said, "I sure do like these things." He leaned on the counter, staring at her. "Do you like them, or is your favorite still horehound drops?"

"I like sugar sticks as well as I like horehound."

He held the second sugar stick toward her. "For you." She reached for the stick. Her hand touched his. His eyes stared into hers. For a long moment, they stood, connected by the sugar stick, their fingers brushing, a deep look in their eyes. "Sweet Amanda," he whispered.

The bell above the door tinkled. Mrs. McClain walked in the store and broke the quiet spell. "I best go," Thomas said, and hurried out of the store.

Amanda felt a hot blush creep up her neck, and set the sugar stick next to the envelope he had lain on the counter. "Hello, Mrs. McClain. Can I help you?"

"Yes, I need a bit of lace for a blouse I'm making."

Amanda stepped up the ladder that was leaning by the shelves, pulled the bobbins of lace off the high shelf, and set them on the counter. "What size did you need?"

"Inch wide, I think."

"Look at this, it's a little wider than an inch, but it has a really pretty scalloped edge."

"Oh, that is nice. I'll take two yards of it."

Amanda measured off the white lace, cut it, and wrapped it in brown paper. After Mrs. McClain took her package and left, Amanda replaced the bobbins on the shelf. Then, from the counter, she picked up the sugar stick in one hand and the envelope, which was addressed to Elizabeth Avery, in the other. *So,* Amanda thought, *What have we here, the bitter and the sweet?* She wondered what on earth Thomas could have written in response to her mistaken, forged letter. *What did he think? What did he write to her?* Amanda tapped the envelope on the counter. She canceled the stamp and paused just before throwing it into the sack. *Maybe I should look, and see if I caused trouble I didn't mean to.* Another voice in her mind said, *You've made enough trouble already! Are you crazy? Put that letter in the sack and forget about it.*

Amanda heeded the latter voice, dropped the letter into the sack, pulled the strings tight, and tied them in a firm knot. "There you are, ready to go." She set the sack aside and went about her other chores.

She didn't think about the letter again until she was

tucked into bed that night. Once again, the voices argued and tugged inside her head. *Go ahead, you really want to look and see what he said,* one voice said. *Leave it be, leave it be,* the opposing voice demanded. Amanda felt as if her head had been possessed by demons that didn't belong to any part of her. She tossed and turned until dawn lightened the sky. Finally, the first voice won. *Just one little tiny, bitsey peek,* it said as Amanda tiptoed down the stairs in her nightgown. Her eyes were bleary as she tugged at the knots on the mail-sack string. She opened it and reached for the envelope on the top of the pile, and pulled it out of the sack. It was Thomas's letter. She set it aside, pulled the sack strings tight, and tied them. *I'm a thief in my own father's store* she thought, as she grabbed the letter and quickly stole up the stairs to her room.

Her heart pounded, her ears hummed. She lay down and put the envelope under her pillow, then tossed and turned for a while longer. Unable to sleep, she climbed out of bed and washed her face in the basin. Dark circles underscored her eyes. She dressed for school; made her bed; tucked Thomas's letter into her pocket next to Elizabeth's opened, smudged letter, and went downstairs. Her father was seated on a stool at the counter, a cup of coffee before him, studying the ledger books. "Good morning," Amanda said, planting a kiss on his cheek.

"You're up early," he commented. "Didn't you sleep well?"

"No, not too well."

"You don't look good. You're not getting a cold or the flu, are you?"

"No, I just had a little trouble sleeping."

"We have several elixirs on the shelves. One or two of them I'm sure claims to cure sleeplessness. Do you want some breakfast?"

"No, I'm not hungry. I have some work I want to get done at school this morning. I'll see you later." She let herself out of the store and hurried up the street, thinking, *Do they make an elixir for thieves with their pockets full of stolen letters? Will it cure guilt, fear of being caught, and other related symptoms?*

The school morning seemed to drag, the children were restless, and Amanda lacked her usual cheery attitude. At noon recess, Justin McClain fell and scraped his knee. As he cried, Amanda held him in her arms and felt like joining right in and sobbing with him for no other reason than that it would feel good to weep.

When the day finally neared its end, Amanda let her students go home a few minutes early. She sat in the quiet, studying the slates piled on her desk, and began to write a critical remark on Carrie Taneman's slate. Carrie was having so much trouble getting her letters shaped just right. Amanda remembered what a difficult time she had trying to copy Elizabeth's graceful handwriting. She opened her middle desk drawer and lifted the grade ledger. There was Elizabeth's letter to Thomas. Beside it was the newest stolen envelope containing Thomas's latest letter to her. *My goodness, this is a fine pair of hostages,* Amanda thought, chastising herself and closing the drawer. She looked at Carrie's slate again. Picking up the chalk, she whispered, "It's so hard to get it right, isn't it?" In the corner, she wrote, *Keep up the good work.*

Amanda took the grade ledger from the drawer, recorded the day's grades, and stuffed it back on top of the letters in the drawer. She grabbed her shawl and left the school. The train pulled into town. Amanda hurried to the store, grabbed the mail sack, and headed for the station. She handed Mr. Hunter the sack. He put it on the train, and they went inside the station house to get the incoming mail. "I trust you took care of my little matter," he stated, as she followed him.

"Yes, sir, all the mail went out, especially your letter. There's no need for you to call at the store looking for return mail. I can bring it down here. It won't be any trouble. I'm taking the Hendersons their mail, too."

"Has that stubborn fool let his kids go back to school yet?"

"No."

"That's a real shame. If I had kids . . . oh, what do I know. I see his point. But I see the other side, too. I guess it doesn't much matter to me one way or the other if women vote or not."

Amanda grated her teeth and held her tongue. *I am a teacher, I will not discuss my politics with anyone. I must protect my job,* she ordered herself. "I best go, Mr. Hunter. I'll see you later." She left the station house and walked to the mercantile thinking about what Mr. Hunter had said. *But it matters a lot to me,* she thought, going into the mercantile.

After Amanda had sorted the mail and helped with the afternoon customers, she took the Henderson mail and walked up the road to the sawmill.

Jacob was in his shop, planing a board smooth. Amanda watched him for a while, fidgeting and praying he would talk to her. When he finally quit, she asked, "Where's Thomas?"

"I sent him to the mountain to bring in more logs." His voice was short and to the point.

"I brought your mail for you." She held it out like an offering.

Jacob brushed his hands on his pants, stepped toward her, and took it with a scowl. "What's this? Three newspapers? I got someone else's paper by mistake." His voice was cold and uninviting.

"No, you didn't. One is the Leader that didn't come

last time, one is today's Leader, and the third is another free sample of the Eagle." Amanda tried to keep her voice light and conversational, hoping he would at least talk to her.

His voice turned terse and bitter. "I'm having trouble with my eyes and don't have my spectacles. If that's all, I have work. . . ."

Amanda pressed a sore subject, saying, "Jacob, please reconsider letting the children come to school. Please, come to the store. You don't have to buy anything. Just come visit with my father. He misses you very much."

"I want nothing to do with a women's-suffrage sympathizer." Jacob stoked up his anger. "That goes for you, Miss Chappell. Get out of my wood shop."

Amanda quietly slipped out the door. "What an unrelenting, unreasonable, inflexible grouch," she said, and walked down the road. When she came to the intersection of the two streets, she looked at the two rows of neat buildings. Her gaze rested on the livery-barn roof. Jacob's words echoed in her mind. *What was it he had said?* she mused, *'It's not square. It'll fall in by spring.'* Amanda stared at the roof. She back-stepped ten steps, studied the roof, and remembered sitting in Jacob's wagon just after she arrived in Paradise. Jacob had pointed out the roof. She remembered turning around on the seat to see it. Something didn't seem right. But she couldn't put her finger on what exactly it was.

Her hands rested on her hips as her mind wandered over the memories of their grader's camp days. She clearly remembered Jacob standing in the bottom of a ravine, yelling up to the crew that had been placing timbers on a bridge they were building. "It's not level," he yelled. "Measure it, you'll see." The other workers were disgruntled when he insisted they stop and measure to make sure. When they did, the timbers were five inches out of alignment. Jacob was right. If the bridge had been built out of alignment, the heavy weight of the trains on the bridge could have caused a problem or even an accident later.

Amanda wracked her brain. Something else seemed out of alignment. *But what? What wasn't right?* She walked toward the store again. Then it hit her. *Spectacles! That's it!* "Spectacles!" she said aloud. Amanda turned and walked up the street again so she could study the roof. Standing there, she said to herself, "Jacob Henderson used to be able to see if a bridge was level or not from a hundred feet away. Now he can sit in a wagon at the top of a street and tell whether a building has a square roof or not. I know I've never seen him wear a pair of spectacles or squint his eyes to look at anything in my life."

She thought back over the last few days. Jacob was cold and unresponsive when she'd tried to talk about the children coming back to school. But the two times Jacob seemed to get especially impatient, confused, and angry with her, was when she gave him his newspapers. The first time, she could understand his confusion. The mastheads on the Leader and the Eagle were so similar. At first glance, one could mistake the two papers. But today, he looked directly at those papers and mistook them. *No, he completely misread them,* she thought. *What was it he'd said? He forgot his spectacles?*

Amanda looked toward the Henderson house. Through the trees, she caught a glimpse of the sawmill roof. Cupping her hands around her mouth, she yelled into the breeze, "Jacob Henderson, in the past your vision was impeccable. I have never, ever, seen you wear a pair of spectacles. I bet you don't *own* a pair. I'll find out if there is something wrong with your eyes or not, Jacob. You watch me. I suspect one of your problems is something else entirely."

Chapter 10

Sitting at her school desk, Amanda studied the page she had just finished. She compared it to one of six-year-old Joseph Henderson's old writing papers from her files. Her lettering was a fairly good reproduction of his penmanship, except her page contained nonsense and random letters written to look like words in sentences. "If I lose my teaching job over the stunt I'm about to pull, I can always go to work as a forger," she told herself, then folded the paper and put it in her calico skirt pocket. She opened her middle desk drawer and gazed at the stolen letters. She sighed and felt guilty that she had gotten busy with school and other things and hadn't had the gumption to make herself return them yet. "Oh, the messes I've gotten myself into," she told herself. "In such a short time." She shut the drawer, felt the paper in her pocket, then left the building, saying, "I'm getting myself into so much trouble." That thought lingered as she concentrated on the trees that were turning yellow, and the afternoon air that had the distinct smell of autumn, as she walked toward the Hendersons. Amanda wasn't sure of what she was about to do, and worse, didn't know what the repercussions would be. A wary nervousness filled her chest. There was a heaviness to her step as she approached the sawmill.

The Henderson children saw her and ran up the road to meet her. "Amanda," they called. "Did you bring some candy?" Leah asked.

"I didn't bring candy this time, but I will next time," she said, picking up Leah and carrying her for a little bit while the other children gathered around her, saying, "How is school? We miss coming. How are our friends? What are you doing here?"

"I need to talk to your father. Is he in the mill? All by himself?"

The children said, "Yes."

Amanda set Leah to the ground and told them, "I won't be long." She marched into the mill, her insides quivering with nerves. The smell of pine sawdust filled her nostrils. Jacob was sawing a board. She waited until he finished and looked up at her. "Hello, Jacob."

"What are you doing?" he asked, sounding irritated.

"I found a paper that your son, Joseph, wrote at school, and I thought you'd like to see it. It's about you and it's so nice, I thought I'd give it to you." Amanda reached into her skirt pocket. The little voice in her head said, *You can stop right now. You don't have to do this.* Amanda hesitated, then pulled it out and handed it to him.

He took it, put it in his pocket, and said, "Thank you. I'll read it later."

"You can't . . . you . . . can't wait to see how sweet it is. Just take a peek. One little peek." Amanda's palms grew clammy. The air in the dusty mill felt muggy and stifling.

"I don't . . . a . . . gee, I don't have my spectacles," Jacob mumbled.

"You won't need your spectacles—the print is very large."

He hesitated, took the paper out of his pocket, unfolded it, and let his eyes rove over the wording. "That is right nice, isn't it," he said, folding it and handing it to her.

Amanda clenched it in her fist, closed her eyes, and took a deep breath. Now that her suspicions were confirmed, she didn't know quite how to proceed or what to do next. Letting out her breath, she whispered, "I've never seen you wear spectacles, Jacob. I bet you don't even own a pair." Her voice quickened. "There is nothing wrong with your eyes, Jacob Henderson. I've seen you stand a hundred feet from a bridge and tell people it wasn't level, and when they measured it, you were right. You can stand in the street and tell if Cal Taneman's livery-barn roof is square or not." Her voice tensed. Her heart filled with regrettable sorrow. "Jacob, you got in a fight with someone who differed with you on a political issue, you pulled your children out of my school and accused me of polluting their minds because I read them an article out of a newspaper and let them discuss it." Her eyes filled with tears. "How dare you!"

"What are you getting at?" he demanded.

"How can you say I polluted your children's minds when you can't even tell what that newspaper really said or not?"

"What do you mean?" he shouted.

Amanda whispered, "You can't read, Jacob, and I know it."

He stood speechless, then, out of breath, retorted, "Of course I can read." His voice rose to a fevered pitch, "What do you think I am, stupid?" His eyes flashed with indignation.

"Admit it, Jacob."

His eyes filled with anger.

She leveled a gaze into his face. "Do you know what

the worst irony is for me, Jacob? You are the one man in this community who has bitterly spoken out against women having the right to vote. You get to vote, yet you can't even read a ballot.'' Tears streamed down her face. "If I had the right to vote, at least I could read my ballot and know what I'm voting for.''

They stood staring at each other. Hatred filled his eyes. "You have a lot of nerve," he said, his voice low and vicious.

Amanda back-stepped. At the doorway, she braced her feet. "No, Jacob,'' she whispered, tears pouring down her face, "I don't have a lot of nerve. You do.'' She unfolded the crumpled paper in her fist and said, "Joseph didn't write this. I did. It doesn't say anything, it's just random letters.''

"It is not,'' he shouted.

"Ask your children." Amanda dropped the crumpled paper into the sawdust at his feet. His face turned red. He shook with rage. Amanda turned and ran out the door and down the road, her skirt flying. She finally stopped at the schoolhouse and sat on the steps to catch her breath. "This was another stupid move,'' she whispered. "What did it prove? That he can't read? Just as I thought? But nothing else,'' she told herself, stood, and walked toward the mercantile. She watched the livery barn roof as she walked, and thought, *I wasn't wrong. That geezer has a lot of people fooled.* A hollow feeling filled her heart. Earlier, she had thought she would feel a certain satisfaction in being right about Jacob. But now that she was right, she didn't feel any kind of satisfaction at all, just a deep sadness.

The next day after school, Amanda dismissed the children to go home and began wiping the chalkboard with a damp rag when she heard a noise at the door. Turning, she found Jacob standing in the cloakroom, his hat in hand, his face intent. They stared at each other for a while. Finally he said, "Afternoon, Amanda."

"Good afternoon, Jacob." They studied each other, both reluctant to speak first.

"Yesterday, you forgot to take your paper with you," he said, stepping into the schoolroom and handing it to her.

She stepped forward and took it, saying, "That wasn't a very nice thing to do. I'm sorry, I don't know what made me do it."

"There doesn't have to be any harm done," he said, a small laugh in his voice. "There's no need to tell anybody about this. You haven't told anybody, have you?"

Amanda tore up the paper and dropped the pieces on the floor between his feet. "Is that what you're worried about? Who I might tell? That someone else will know? If I were you, Jacob, I'd be worried that my children weren't in school where they should be. I'd be even more worried that I can't read."

"Claire always helps me get by. Always reads the Bible and the newspapers to me. Does all the figures and adding and subtracting for us. We've gotten along pretty good."

"What will you do if Claire ever isn't around? It worked when you were following construction jobs and on the move all the time. But you're in one place now. People are more likely to find out about it."

"Not if nobody tells."

"Yes, they will."

"Only if you choose to tell."

"Don't fool yourself, Jacob. If I never tell another soul, someone else will figure it out just like I did, sooner or later. What will you do then? What about your children? They need to be in school. They can learn to read from the Bible all right, and I'm not shorting Claire's ability to teach the children well. But coming to school is more than just reading and doing figures. It's learning how to get along with other children who think, act, and are different. They need that, so when they grow up, they'll know how to get along with others. School is a chance to learn about more than what's in your own front yard. It's about learning to see beyond yourself."

"Are you going to tell?" he asked.

Amanda turned to the chalkboard and angrily swiped at the chalk-writing with the rag. "Are you going to let your children come back to school?"

"I reckon that could be arranged."

She stopped the angry swipes. "Really? That's good, I'm glad. It's what I want you to do for the children. This is what you have to do for me . . ." She finished wiping the chalk from the board. He twisted his dusty hat between his rough hands. She folded the rag and set it in the chalk tray. "Please, learn to read. When I get old enough to vote, Jacob, and can't because I'm a woman, at least give me the comfort of knowing you can read the ballot when you vote."

"What do you mean?"

"What part of that do you not understand? I'm telling you to *learn to read!* That's the price if you want my silence."

"How am I gonna do that? I can't ask Claire to teach me. What would she think of her poor stupid husband?"

"I'm a teacher. I teach. You are not a stupid man, Jacob Henderson. Being unable to read doesn't make you stupid. It just means you haven't had time to learn."

"I musta been eight years old when I went to work hauling freight with my papa. Been working hard ever since. Do you understand that?" He swiped at the tears glistening in his eyes. "I ain't afraid of working hard.

But lookin' stupid to other people, that scares me plum to death." He turned and placed his hand on the doorknob. "You won't tell anybody I'm learning to read?"

"No one." She addressed his broad back and straight shoulders. "I help my father in the store on mail-delivery days. The store is real busy on those days, and with him digging the root cellar, he's even more busy. But the other days, I'll be staying late after school just in case someone wants to stop by and learn to read or something. I promise, no one will ever know."

"You're asking too much," he said, opening the door and stepping into the afternoon sun. The door clicked shut. Amanda went to her desk and slumped into her chair. She had never talked to an adult in such a manner. It left her insides shaking and her heart thumping. She sighed, straightened the children's slates that were sitting on her desk, then left the school.

Feeling like a traitor, she walked toward home. There was no triumph in having discovered Jacob's weakness and fears. After all, she had always thought of him as friend and family. There was no joy in remembering the defeated look on his face. Amanda shuddered and regretted her newfound knowledge. *It didn't change a thing anyway,* she thought, her stomach hurting.

The next morning she arrived at school, graded the slates, and set them on the desks at each child's place. She hated that only half of the seats had a slate sitting on its companion desk. She didn't, for one minute, let herself hope that Jacob would let the children return to school. He would never come to her to learn to read. His pride was wounded. One thing she instinctively knew, *You don't hurt a man's pride.* She wished she hadn't done what she'd done. *How do I make it right?* she wondered, and wrote the day's arithmetic problems on the chalkboard. When she turned from the board,

Leah Henderson stood at the classroom door, smiling. "Did I scare you, Miss Amanda?"

"Leah? What are you doing?"

"Are you glad to see me?"

Amanda ran toward the child, scooped her up, and spun her around, hugging her close. "Am I glad to see you? Yes! Sweetie, what are you doing here?"

"I'm at school."

Happy tears filled Amanda's eyes. "Just you? Where are your bothers and sister?"

"Pa said as soon as we finish our chores, we can get on to school this morning. I got mine done fast. Those slowpokes will be along soon."

"What did your father say?"

"Nothing, he just said, 'get your chores done and get yourselves to school this morning.' Are you excited, Amanda?"

"Oh boy, am I excited!" She hugged the little girl.

Footsteps clumped up the steps, and the rest of the Henderson children trooped into the school. "We're back, Miss Amanda," Zeek, Jeremiah, and Samuel shouted.

Amanda set Leah down and gathered all of them in her arms. "I'm so glad," she said, her heart soaring. "I couldn't be happier."

Within the next few minutes, the McClain and Taneman children arrived.

Amanda stood before her class and welcomed all the children to school. Wanting to make light of the past situation, she didn't mention the fact that part of the children had been gone for a while. Instead she emphasized how wonderful it was to be together and have their school complete again. "Now put your slates in front of you, and let's do our sums." Amanda smiled to herself as their heads bowed over their slates to work at the problems she had written on the board. She walked around the classroom silently watching them work, looking over their shoulders, pointing out errors and giving quiet words of encouragement. Placing her hand on each child's shoulder as she walked around, she said a silent prayer of thanksgiving for having that which was broken made whole again. Her family, her little chicks, were home once more.

By noon, the children had worked hard. She let them out early for lunch. Grabbing their sweaters and lunch pails, they ran outside, shouting and yelling, "Baseball! David brought his bat. Come on, Miss Amanda, let's play ball."

The children divided themselves into their original teams. Amanda reminded them of their special school rules. "An older child can run the bases for a younger child. No name-calling. Ties at bases automatically go players who have to run in skirts." She stood on the pitcher's mound, pitching slow and easy for the younger players, hard and fast for the more skilled, older players. They laughed, played, and cheered for each other. At the end of the game, the score was tied, and no one seemed to mind.

When school ended, the children hung back before going home. "Are we going to play the big baseball game to decide what to name our teams?" they asked.

Amanda marveled that while the Henderson children had been gone for several days, it seemed like their absence had never happened. The day had simply picked up the rhythm and laughter that had been there on the very first day of school.

"Let me think about it tonight," Amanda told them and sent them on their way. She gave a contented sigh, and stood on the steps waving to them as they went their separate paths toward home. "I love you all," she whispered, then stepped back into the school. Amanda straightened the desks and benches, picked up a piece of paper from the floor, took the broom from the cloak-room, and swept the floor. While she was bent over sweeping the dirt into a dustpan, she heard a heavy step in the cloakroom. Looking up, she saw Jacob standing, hat in hand, in a pool of sunlight that was coming through the windows and shining in a bright spot on the floor.

"Jacob?"

"Afternoon."

"Thank you for letting the children come to school. It is so nice when they're here." Amanda crossed her fingers and silently hoped that he wasn't going to change his mind. "Jacob, I was awful hard on you the other day. The important thing is that the children are in school. You don't need to learn to read. I won't tell anyone you can't, I promise."

"I'm not a man to go back on my word," he said, and hung his hat on one of the coat hooks. "I reckon this is going to take some time. We best get started. Where do you sit those who need to learn to read?"

"Right here," she pulled a bench away from a desk, took a beginning reader book from the shelf and sat beside him.

She remembered back to when she was a girl in the grader's camp. Jacob had often disciplined her along with his own children, saying, "You kids, don't fight. It ain't right to be fighting. You kids, be nice to each other, or I'll sit you down on a rock until you can get along. Be kind, I won't tolerate meanness. Nobody tolerates meanness. Wash up and don't forget to get behind your ears, dirt likes to hide behind those ears." He had been the teacher of so many of life's little in-structions. Amanda opened the book. Now that the roles were reversed, she doubted her ability to be half the teacher Jacob had been.

Chapter 11

The yellowing leaves on the cottonwood trees surrounding the baseball diamond fluttered in the slight breeze. The sun stood overhead in the azure sky and an autumn cool touched the air. It was a Saturday made for baseball. Amanda tugged on her straw-hat brim. She eyeballed the players in the outfield and the other team at home base. The school's baseball game had quickly become Paradise's first official civic event. All the town's people, even those from the outlying areas who didn't have children in school, were seated on quilts on the outskirts of the field. Inside the school building were hampers and baskets full of fried chicken, jars of tangy pickles, aromatic apple pies, and jugs of tart lemonade.

The rocks Amanda had been using for bases were replaced with flour sacks full of sand from the creek. Even Mr. Hunter had left the train depot, and sat with Amanda's father and the Hendersons on their quilt. After his first reading lesson, Jacob had gone down to the mercantile to talk to William. They had mended their differences, Jacob and the others were shopping at the store again, and they sat together as if the disagreement had never taken place.

The children voted and made Thomas an honorary member of the school so he could play. Then they drew straws to see which team got Thomas and which got Amanda. Thomas could run faster, but Amanda could pitch with a deadly aim.

Thomas gave his first batter, Justin McClain, some last-minute encouragement before Justin stepped up to home base. Amanda rolled the ball between her palms and prepared to wing it toward the catcher. She studied her team again. Some of them had taken old woolen socks, cut five holes in the toes of them, and put them over their hands with their fingers sticking out through the holes to help protect their hands from the hard, fast balls. Amanda wiped her palms on her skirt and let the first ball fly. The game was under way.

When the first inning ended, Amanda's team was ahead by one run. Amanda thought it was interesting to watch the crowd. The students were divided up so that children from each family were playing on each team. The parents ended up having to cheer for both teams equally. The residents without children cheered for both teams and were happy to be out in the sunshine, taking a day off from work and cares.

The game played out with cheering, laughter, ups and downs. Sweat dotted the brows of the players as Amanda's team stepped up for their last turn at bat. It was the bottom of the last inning. The score was tied. The first batter struck out, and the second was put out at first base. It was Amanda's turn at bat. She took a couple of practice swings and approached the sandbag. Cocking her arms into place, she leveled her gaze at the pitcher's mound. Thomas, who was pitching, stood and stared at her. Their eyes locked in a silent conversation that had nothing to do with fly balls, strikes, or bases. Amanda's temples throbbed as she tried to guess what his gaze meant. *Don't do this to me, Thomas Lew-*

ellen, she thought. *Don't play games with me or my heart.* She hoped her eyes were telling him to stop it, but knew that the eyes always give away the feelings of the heart. *He has to know that no matter how hard I try, I can't make myself stop loving him. My eyes must tell him that.*

Without taking his gaze off of her, he let the ball fly. It sailed true and straight over home base. "Strike," everyone called. Amanda stepped away from the base, and tapped at the ground with the bat. *Don't look at him. He's doing that on purpose,* she thought. Her teammates gathered around her with hope-filled eyes. Amanda was their best chance to score and win the game.

Amanda could feel the tension build. She stepped up to the base again. *Don't look him in the eye,* she told herself, *don't let him do this to you.* This time she refused to look at him, and watched his hands and the ball. It came wide, outside the base. "Ball," everyone shouted. "One ball, one strike." The ball flew back to the pitcher's mound. Amanda gripped the bat, angry with herself and with Thomas. She took a deep breath and let the anger flow through her. She leveled a steady, mad gaze at him. *You love her, not me,* she thought, *I hate you for that, Thomas.*

He gave her a crooked smile and leaned over to glance at his outfield, then back at her. His gaze seemed to snicker at hers. The ball came fast. Amanda squeezed her hands and swung with all her anger and might. The crack of the bat against the ball was so sound and so sharp, no one had to watch it fly to know it was over the trees. The spectators jumped to their feet to watch it fly. Everyone gasped, then cheered.

Amanda amazed herself as she watched the ball fly, grabbed up her skirts, and ran to first. She rounded second when the children caught up with the ball and heaved it toward third. Thomas ran from the mound to meet her as she passed third. The children on her team were shouting "Run, Amanda, run! Hurry up! Run!" The other team was yelling, "Get the ball! Hurry, get it!"

She headed for home base and heard heavy footsteps behind her. Looking back, she saw Thomas hot on her trail, but he didn't have the ball. He lunged for her. She sidestepped him. He still followed, a mischievous grin on his face. He reached to grab her again. She pulled off her hat and threw it at him. Half of the children and the crowd yelled, "Run, Amanda, run!" The other half yelled, "Catch her, Thomas!"

Amanda ran out of the baseline and tried to avoid him, but he followed. Her skirt flapped around her legs in a tangle as he scooped her up and ran toward home with her in his arms. Amanda screamed and squirmed, but his strong arms held her close. When they reached home base, the children were there with the ball. Thomas laughed as the children surrounded them, shouting, "Who won? Did we still win?" Thomas swung Amanda around, laughing, then gently set her on the ground. She braced herself against him for a moment, her cheek on his chest, to regain her balance and catch her breath. "Whew," she said, looking up at him. Their eyes met again. His held a gentle tenderness and a lot of laughter. Amanda's heart melted. *I could have you look at me like this forever,* she thought. The children jostled them and demanded, "Who won?" "That wasn't fair to do, was it?"

Thomas gallantly bowed. "It was my fault. Without my assistance, Amanda would have had an official home run. Your team picks its new name."

"Paradise Knickerbockers!" they all yelled.

Thomas picked up the bat and touched each of the team members on the shoulder. "I dub thee a Paradise

Knickerbocker," he said to each. When he came to Amanda, he touched her on the shoulder with the bat, and their eyes met again. This time Amanda saw something different in them. It was as if he were really looking at her for the first time and seeing her. "I dub thee," he whispered, "a Paradise Knicker—"

"Name us now," the children on his own team chanted. "We're the Paradise Six, and we'll get you next time, Knickerbockers." Thomas seemed to drag his eyes away from her when he turned to name each of the players on his team. He looked like a king knighting his knights in honor and splendor.

The parents gathered around and complimented all the players for a great and entertaining game. Claire Henderson said, "There'll be fried chicken in a jiffy."

The women scurried into the schoolhouse to set out the food and serve it from a table under a cottonwood tree. They demanded that Amanda be the guest of honor and have her plate filled first. Amanda piled on a piece of chicken, a buttered yeast roll, and a piece of apple pie. "Here's some lemonade," Abe McClain's wife said, handing her a glass. The men filled their plates next, then the children, then the other women. Amanda and her father sat in a shady spot under a cottonwood tree near the school. Thomas came and sat with them. Everyone else gathered in little groups not far from them. It seemed that they had just started to eat when the children finished eating and ran off to play tag.

Jacob Henderson and Cal Taneman steered clear of each other. They were polite to each other, but neither overly friendly, nor openly nasty to each other. After Cal had punched Jacob, the two men had been careful to keep a distance from each other. For the sake of the children, they seemed to have left their political differences at home for the day. Even though Jacob, his family, and his friends were back to shopping at the mercantile again, you never saw Jacob and Cal Taneman walking down the same side of the street or in the store at the same time. They stayed away from each other, but at least the tensions had eased, and Amanda was grateful for that.

As people finished eating, they lay back on the grass to doze in the sun or visit quietly. Thomas toyed with the hem of Amanda's skirt. She didn't know whether to pull it out of his reach or not. She remembered the stolen letters in her desk and blushed. Thomas laughed, "What's the blush all about?"

Amanda shrugged, and thought, *If you only knew.* "Nothing," she said, and lowered her eyes.

William Chappell cleared his throat and said "Amanda, would you gather the children, please? I have a surprise for them."

Amanda stepped into the school and took her bell from the desk. She stood on the steps and rang it. The children ran from all the corners of the playground. "Go see Mr. Chappell," she told them, "he says he has a surprise for you."

She joined Thomas and William under the tree. The children gathered around William as he unwrapped a package. "Sugar sticks!" the children shouted. "Yippee! Candy!"

William handed them out to the children. They thanked him and ran off to play. Amanda smiled as she watched. Thomas said, "You love your students, don't you?"

"I love them very much," she said, her eyes meeting his, their gazes matching.

"I can tell," he said.

He almost said something else when William handed each of them a sugar stick, too. "For the youngsters and the not so young," he said.

Thomas stuck the candy his in his mouth, tasted it,

and pulled it out. "I don't think I'll ever get too old for sugar sticks." He looked at Amanda again, "I love them, don't you?" he whispered.

Amanda felt herself blush and refused to look at him.

His voice teased, "Come on, Amanda, tell me everything you love."

Amanda was saved from having to muster an answer when Claire walked over and said, "I best get on home. The cow needs milking, and the younguns need to chore."

Amanda jumped up and said, "Let me help you gather your dishes and things."

Quickly, the other women followed suit, and were soon packing dishes into the hampers and baskets. They took pity on Mr. Hunter, the bachelor stationmaster, and heaped a plate with leftover chicken and apple pie for him. He thanked the women profusely, took his plate, and left.

Before long, everyone but Thomas and the Hendersons had left. Claire took the children and went home. Jacob Henderson and Amanda's father sat on the steps of the school and talked about the new root cellar and how best to set the braces and joists for it. Thomas offered to carry Amanda's basket with her empty pie plate and dishes. "You don't have to, I can get it," she told him.

"I want to," he said, taking the basket from her.

They walked toward the store, talking and laughing about the game.

When they arrived at the door of the mercantile, Thomas said, "Thank you, Amanda, for the nicest day I have had in a very long time. You are really a good friend." Amanda felt a stab in her heart and reached for her basket. He pulled it away, saying, "I'll take it in for you."

She opened the door, and they went into the mercantile. He set the basket on the counter. Amanda reached for it. His hands covered hers. She refused to look at him, her heart aching.

"Sweet Amanda, what's the matter?" He tipped her chin up so that she had to look at him. "What could possibly be wrong with the best home-run-hitting, fastball-pitching baseball player west of the Mississippi River? Come on, smile for me."

Tears filled Amanda's eyes. "Thomas, don't say we're friends, then turn around and flirt with me. Don't play games with me."

"What do you mean?" His fingers gently traced the outline of her chin.

"You're playing games with my heart, Thomas. I beg you, please don't."

He studied her for a moment, wiped her tears with the tip of his thumb, then whispered, "What on earth makes you think that?"

Amanda stepped away from him. *What am I supposed to say? I think so, Thomas, because I've been stealing your mail lately?* "Are you, Thomas? Be honest with me. Are you free to give your heart to me?"

He pulled his hands away from hers. "I'm sorry, Amanda, I can't answer that right now." He turned and walked out the door, the bell tinkling behind him.

Chapter 12

When Monday came, Amanda walked to school and prepared the classroom for the day. She cleaned the chimney on the oil lamp and straightened the desks. She looked at the slates with the children's penmanship exercises, graded them, placed them at each child's place, then sat at her desk and reviewed the grades in the grade ledger. The Henderson children were catching up nicely from the school they had missed. All in all, she was very pleased with her little school and all of her students. She opened her narrow, middle desk drawer to put the grade ledger into its place.

Thomas's letters were sitting in the drawer. Amanda shuddered, took the letters and threw them in the stove. As she slammed the stove shut with a metallic clink, she realized, as warm as it had been, she probably wouldn't be lighting a fire for a while. She retrieved the letters and stuffed them in the desk drawer, saying, "If you love her, Thomas, I'm not going to make it any easier for you." She threw the grade ledger on top of the letters and slammed the drawer shut. "For a while, anyway," she said, "that'll teach you to play with my heart."

Amanda banished all thoughts about the letters from her mind when her students arrived for the day. When they played baseball at noon, Amanda ended up pitching for both teams. The Henderson children told her that Thomas had gone to the mountains for more logs for the sawmill and wouldn't be able to play ball with them for a week or so. Amanda breathed a sigh of relief, walked to the pitcher's mound, and wiped her hands on her dress as she prepared to pitch. "Hey, batter batter," she called, beginning to enjoy the game.

After school, Amanda rushed to the mercantile to help her father. She grabbed the mail sack and hurried to the train station to trade the outgoing sack for the incoming sack. Mr. Hunter hovered rather close to her as she went out the door. Amanda had the feeling that he wanted her to open the sack right then to see if he had received a letter. She reminded him, "It won't be proper, Mr. Hunter, if I open the sack now. If someone catches us shuffling through the letters outside of the post office, it will look bad."

He huffed and puffed and stammered, "Why, I know that, of course I do. Messing with the U.S. mail is serious business, I always say that, yes sir."

"I promise to keep my word, Mr. Hunter. If there is anything for you, I'll keep it quiet and bring it down here as soon as I can."

"I wasn't expecting anything in particular," he said, following her outside to the edge of the platform. "That was a fine ball game Saturday, yes sir. I surely enjoyed it. You have a real fine school, Miss Amanda."

"Thank you, Mr. Hunter. I'll see you later."

Amanda hurried to the mercantile where customers were already waiting for their mail. She sorted the newspapers and magazines and handed them to the waiting patrons. She turned to the letters and sorted them. Three letters were addressed to Mr. Hunter.

Amanda quietly slipped them into her apron pocket. There was one to her from Laura. "What does it say, Amanda?" Cal Taneman asked.

"Let's see," said Amanda, opening the letter and reading aloud, *"Dearest Amanda, I only have a short time to write. It was good to hear that things are going well for you in your school. My teaching is getting easier. The father of one of those ornery, older boys found a vein of gold in the hills and took his son out of school to help him dig for it. The other boy went with them. Things are going better, but I fear because of the circus I had with those two boys, it put all of my other students woefully behind. I will have to work very hard to get them caught up to where they should be. I worry for the two boys. What will happen to them in a few years when the gold plays out, and they have no education?*

Do you remember our pact to never marry or fall in love until we have won the right to vote? I'm not sure it was a prudent promise to make. I am willing to forget that promise. Just in case you've fallen in love, or met someone, or something like that. Not that I have fallen in love or anything, just that one can never tell what the future may bring. One really shouldn't make promises against the future, don't you think? Write soon. Love, Laura. P.S. Have you heard, Colonel William H. Bright from here has been elected to the Territorial Legislature. Ben Sheeks was also elected. I personally think Colonel Bright is our best hope to get a suffrage bill introduced. He was in attendance at the tea party I previously wrote to you about. He is a very nice man. Ben Sheeks, however, is an abrasive, argumentative, sarcastic lawyer. I don't much care for him. He is a man's man and thinks the world should be a man's world. He will never vote for a suffrage bill."

Amanda refolded the letter. No one offered any comment on the news. Cal Taneman said, "Maybe a body should go get some of that gold they're finding in South Pass City.''

"So few find gold," Abe McClain said. "My brother tried to strike it rich in the California gold rush of forty-nine. He finally made more money selling pickaxes and gold pans to incoming miners than he ever made scratching in the dirt.''

Amanda was grateful that the discussion had turned to gold and different gold-discovery stories. No one seemed to want to discuss women's suffrage. She wondered if everyone was afraid of being punched in the mouth and simply avoided the subject.

While the others talked about gold prospecting, Amanda helped her father wait on customers. She took molasses from the shelf and added a skein of yellow embroidery floss and a tin of tea for Mrs. McClain. While she measured some sugar out of the barrel and weighed it, the matronly banker's wife whispered, "When you write back to your friend, tell her that you can never make promises against the future. When your heart says follow, you can't do anything but that. No one knows where the future will call your heart. Sounds to me like she's in love. Tell her to follow her heart. No matter what politics say, no matter what else happens, if it's true love, you can't go wrong.''

Amanda quietly nodded and wrapped up the sugar with the rest of the items, and said, "Thank you, Mrs. McClain.'' She lowered her voice and said, "I'll tell her that next time I write.''

"Are you ready to go, Mama?" Abe McClain asked his wife.

"Yes, dear.'' She took her package off of the counter. He took it from her. They turned and went to the door. He reached to open it for her. Amanda stepped to the window and watched them. He gently placed his hand at the small of her back. They talked. She smiled,

113

and he laughed at something she said. *How like dancers they are,* Amanda thought as she watched them. Walking up the street, they seemed to know each other's next move. His hand went to her elbow as she stepped from the boardwalk, the package went under his other arm as they linked hands. Amanda envied their comfort and ease with each other. *They certainly make it look easy,* she thought, turning away from the window to go help another customer.

After a while, everyone had been helped. Amanda told her father that she was slipping out for a minute. He was deep in conversation with Cal Taneman and simply nodded his balding head.

Amanda walked to the train station. "Mr. Hunter. Mr. Hunter," she called when she poked her head in the door.

He came downstairs from his upstairs living quarters. "Miss Amanda?"

"Guess what, Mr. Hunter? You got some mail." She handed him the envelopes addressed in feminine handwriting.

His eyes widened and his hands shook as he took them from her. Amanda guessed that he didn't want her around while he read them. "I'll see you later, Mr. Hunter." He seemed not to hear her as he studied each envelope. Amanda smiled to herself and slipped out the door. "I hope you find what you're looking for," she whispered, and quietly closed the door.

The next day, after the children left school for the afternoon, Amanda straightened the schoolroom while she waited to see if Jacob Henderson would come for a reading lesson. She heard his boots clump on the front steps. When he came in, he had his big family Bible tucked under his arm. "I read from that book you gave me yesterday, and by golly, I figured it all out, I can read now," he said, taking a seat.

Amanda sat next to him. "Let me hear you, Jacob. Let's see how you did."

Jacob opened the Bible to the first page and read, "In the beginning God created. . . ."

He read for a while, his voice clear and smooth. Amanda sensed something wasn't right. She reached over and flipped the Bible open to another section. "That was beautiful, Jacob. But the Psalms are my favorite. Try one of them." She pointed. "Read this one right here for me."

"Umm . . . a . . ."

"Need your spectacles, Jacob?"

He blushed and shut the book. "Amanda . . ."

"Jacob Henderson, what are you trying to pull? I bet you've heard Claire read that Bible so many times, you have it memorized, don't you? That is, until someone opens it in a random place." He blushed a deep scarlet. "Jacob, you can fool yourself and others, but now that I know you can't read, you can't fool me." She stood, hands on hips. "I never said this would be easy. You don't have to learn to read. That wasn't part of the deal. Just let your children come to school so they can. Tell me something, Jacob, if something ever happens to Claire, who will read, write, and cipher for you? If it's going to be your children, you better make sure they know how to do it well."

Anger filled his face. He breathed heavily and stomped toward the door. "I don't need none of your sass, Missy."

Just before he opened the door, Amanda called, "Come back when you're really ready to learn. I'll be here."

He stormed out the door, mounted his horse, and galloped away from the school.

Amanda wondered if she had gone too far, said too much. Shaking, she picked up her shawl and prayed she hadn't made him too mad.

The next day, she was deeply grateful to see all the Henderson children in their places when school started. That afternoon, when school was over and the children left, she looked up from the slates she was grading and was surprised to find Jacob standing in the doorway.

"How are you?" she asked, her voice tentative.

"I'm here . . ." he hesitated and waited, his mouth working to form the words. "I'm here, because I don't know how to read or properly sign my name. I want . . . I would like to be able to really write my name instead of doodling some mark and pretending it's a signature. When I do sign a paper or something, I'd like to be able to read it and make sure it really says what they tell me it says. My old habits have served me well. I got by without any learning up until now, but I know it won't be enough from now on. It's hard, Amanda, to admit to someone that you're stupid."

"Jacob, I refuse to teach stupid people. I can't. You might as well go home."

His mouth dropped open. "What do you mean?"

"I don't believe there is any such thing as a stupid person, Jacob. The fact that you fooled people for such a long time tells me just how smart you are. You have to believe you are not stupid, or I can't teach you a thing. We'll be wasting each other's time."

He studied her for a while and said, "Do you really think so?"

"I know so. Now, what's it going to be, do you want to do this or not? Learning to read will make you feel stupid at first. It will be frustrating to try to learn new words, but if you struggle along, pretty soon it will get easier and easier until it will be just like drinking water, and you won't think twice about it when you go to read something. It's really quite magical."

"Fine, Amanda. Now, please, teach this stupi . . . no, not stupid." He took a heavy breath and exhaled. "Please, teach this ignorant man how to read. I want to know how to do the magic."

Chapter 13

The weather changed, turning from Indian-summer warm to chilly, near-winter fall. Snow fell on the distant mountains and stayed, capping them with white. The days flitted past, like the leaves falling from the cottonwood trees. Amanda's time was full of teaching school, working in the store, and helping her father. When mid-October came, her life had a comfortable, satisfying rhythm filled with a sense of accomplishment. She had ordered pretty floral wallpaper and pasted it to the plaster walls in the living quarters above the store. With Claire Henderson's help and her treadle sewing machine, Amanda made lacy curtains and hung them in the windows. She dug through some of the boxes stashed in the upstairs storeroom, found her mother's old things, and took out the delicate china vases and dishes, dusted them, and set them on the tables and shelves. When Amanda finished, the upstairs rooms had a bright, homey comfort.

At school, her students were learning quickly and, more importantly, with joy. When the weather allowed, they played baseball at noon recess, both teams winning about an equal number of games. Thomas joined them for a game now and then. His days were busy with working at the sawmill and hauling pine logs down from the mountain in a heavy wagon. He and Jacob were worried that once the heavy winter snows hit, they might not be able to get up on the mountain for a few months. They were working like busy ants to build up a winter supply of logs to have on hand to cut for locomotive fuel and to use as lumber.

Amanda was glad that Thomas's work kept him away, and he didn't come to school to play ball too often. When he did show up teasing and flirting, she was reminded of the letters hidden in her desk drawer. Her heart always filled with guilt, and she constantly chastised herself. It seemed like the longer she put off taking care of the letters, the harder it was to do it.

Amanda's greatest joy came from the private reading lessons she was giving to Jacob Henderson. Jacob proved to be far more impatient than her younger, regular students, but he was also quick and keen. After the first few, frustrating lessons, she thought he would quit. During one difficult session, he stormed out of the school cussing. Two days later, he came back and told her that he had stayed up all night working on the difficult passage. When he read it aloud perfectly, he slapped the desk with his palms and shouted, "There! You can't get the best of me." Amanda clapped and quickly hid the joyful tears that filled her eyes. If anything, she realized how much Jacob was teaching her. Watching him struggle made her realize how hard and difficult it was to learn new things. She vowed never to take for granted her younger students and their struggles to accomplish the things she demanded of them.

One blustery evening, after supper, Amanda sat at the small table which usually held the checkerboard, next to the potbellied stove, in the mercantile. By the light of the oil lamp, she worked on lesson plans and writing evaluations of her students for their parents while she enjoyed the warmth of the fire in the stove. Her father sat at his desk working on the ledgers. Amanda heard a tapping at the door and went to open it. Claire Henderson stood outside the door, a heavy shawl wrapped about her. "Can I have a word with you, Amanda?"

"Come in by the fire, for heaven's sake. It's chilly out there."

Claire stepped into the store, then noticed William sitting at his desk. She fidgeted and mumbled, "I thought you were alone, Amanda. We can step outside and talk."

William looked at Amanda and raised his eyebrows, "You ladies, sit by the fire. I have to go upstairs and count inventory. I'll get out of your way." He took his book and went upstairs.

"Sit down, Claire. Can I get you some coffee or make some tea?"

"No, thank you." Claire's usually bubbly voice was dismal. Her gray-streaked hair strayed out of the usually tidy bun.

"Is something wrong, Claire? Are the children all right? Is it Jacob?"

Tears poured out of Claire's eyes. Amanda grabbed a brand-new men's bandanna off the shelf and handed it to Claire. "What's wrong?"

"As if you don't know," Claire said, her voice full of pain.

"As if I don't know . . . ?"

"Do you think I don't know?"

"Know what?" Concern filled Amanda's voice.

"About you . . ." Claire pointed an accusing finger, "and my husband."

"What?" The air left Amanda's lungs, she couldn't get her breath as the realization of what Claire was saying came clear.

"I know you have designs on him, and I know he's been slipping away from work, sneaking up to the school to see you."

A horrible realization filled Amanda's heart. She knelt at Claire's knee, "That is not what it is. Claire, don't you know you are the very last person on this earth that I would ever hurt? I'm so sorry, if for a single minute, you were led to think anything of the kind."

"I may be a silly old, useless woman, but I am not stupid."

"Let me explain. A few weeks ago, I found out that Jacob can't read. First it was by accident, then I tricked him so I would know for sure." Claire stopped crying and stared at Amanda. "When I confronted him, we made a deal. I promised not to tell a soul, and he agreed to let your children come back to school. Then I went one step further and bullied him into learning to read. On the days that I don't handle the mail for my father, I stay after school and give Jacob reading lessons."

Claire buried her face in the bandanna. The embarrassed blush of red that colored her neck, ears, and face nearly matched the bandanna color. Amanda wrapped her arms around Claire, saying, "I love you and Jacob and the children. You are my extended family. I would never do anything to hurt any of you."

"I feel so foolish," Claire said, wiping her face. "How could I think such a thing to begin with? Just imagine. No wonder he changed his mind and let the children go back to school! You must think I am an awful, jealous, old woman."

"I think nothing of the kind, Claire."

"I know Jacob can't read. I've always known. But when I look at him, I don't see that. I see a handsome, strong, hardworking man, not a man who can't read."

Amanda smiled to herself. She had never thought of Jacob, with his stout build and graying hair, as being handsome. To Claire, he was nothing but handsome. *That's how it should be,* Amanda thought, thinking about them. *And that's how I want to be.*

"I love him so much," Claire added, "I always forget about the reading because we get by just fine. When he was slipping away in the afternoons, I couldn't guess why. So I followed him and found out he was going to the school. You can imagine what thoughts filled my crazy head."

"I understand, Claire. And I understand how jealousy can make you think and do crazy things. We've all done some stupid or silly thing because of jealousy and love. It's a dangerous combination."

"Surely not you, Amanda."

"Oh, Claire, if you only knew." She blushed and couldn't make herself say anymore. "Let's don't talk about how stupid we've been. Would you be more comfortable if I quit giving Jacob lessons?"

"No! Please don't do that." Her voice was emphatic. "I want him to know how to read. I beg you, don't tell him we had this talk."

"I won't tell, Claire, trust me."

"Please, forgive me. How could I think the things I thought about you and my husband?" She shook her head and shuddered. "You must think I'm a horrible person."

"No, I don't, Claire."

"I worry sometimes that Jacob will want to find a woman who is younger, prettier, and smarter than me. For a while, I've been worried that something I did might have turned him away from me."

"What could you have done to turn him away from you?"

"I made him settle down and stay in one place. Ever since we were married, we've followed construction work. Our family has lived in a tent most of our lives.

I'm getting older, and I'm tired of it. I told Jacob I couldn't wander here and there anymore, and that I wasn't spending another winter in a tent. I wanted a roof over my head and four solid walls around me. Jacob said he didn't know if he could do that. I said, fine, you go do whatever you want to. The children and I are staying put. When the railroad people came and said they were building this town, I told Jacob I wanted to come here. He grudgingly agreed. When we first arrived, Jacob said, 'what do you think, Claire?' I said, 'it looks like Paradise to me.' "

"Is that why this place is called Paradise?"

"Yes," said Claire, smiling. "On the spot, we built our house. Ever since, I've been hoping and praying Jacob will be happy settled here. It's hard to take the rambling out of a rambling, traveling man."

"Claire, Jacob loves you. In fact he didn't want me to tell anyone, especially you, that he is taking reading lessons. He didn't want you to think he is less than he is."

"I would never think such a thing," she retorted, pulling her shawl around her. "I best go. My family will wonder what on earth happened to me. I told them I was coming over to help you with a sewing project."

"I'll keep your secret."

"Amanda, if you don't mind my asking," her voice softened, "how is he doing with his lessons?"

"Claire, you'd be proud of him. He's doing so well. Last week, I started teaching him to write and recognize the cursive alphabet. He learns new words like a thirsty horse sucks up water from a trough. The fact that he is learning so fast tells me he has a sharp, fine mind."

"I knew that!" She held her head high, walked to the door, turned, and said, "How can I ever thank you?"

Amanda opened the door for her, saying, "You can't, Claire, because after all this, I would still be indebted to you for standing in for my mother, comforting me when I hurt myself, or someone hurt my feelings, and for all the things you taught me. You kept up my reading skills and schooling back when we were living in the grader's camp. I couldn't have finished normal school so fast if you hadn't done that. I haven't begun to repay you for all you've done for me and my father over the years."

Amanda put her arms around Claire, and they held each other for a moment. Claire pulled away and said, "Let's not keep accounts on who owes who what, or who did what for whom. I don't like to keep accounts, I just do what needs to be done. Isn't that how it should be?"

"Absolutely. Good night, Claire." The older woman stepped out into the blustery, bright moonlight and disappeared up the street. Amanda returned to her work, barely picked up her pen, and heard another light tapping at the door. She hurried to open it, saying, "Claire, did you forget something?"

"It's not Claire," a male voice said, and stepped out of the shadows.

"Mr. Hunter?" she said to the stationmaster. "What on earth are you doing out there in the dark?"

He stepped into the mercantile, shivered, and went to hold his hands over the warm stove. "I was chilled down, but good. I didn't think Mrs. Henderson would ever finish her business and leave."

"You've been standing out there all this time?"

"Where is your father?"

"Upstairs. I'll get him for you."

"Don't do that, it's you I want to see."

"Me?"

He reached into his jacket pocket and pulled out an envelope. "Here."

"What is this?" Amanda asked, taking it from him.

124

"What does it look like?"

Amanda felt a little silly. "Of course, it's a letter . . ." Over the last few weeks, a flurry of letters had passed between him and three ladies. Amanda had noticed that the correspondence had been reduced to a flurry of letters between him and one woman. True to her word, Amanda had kept quiet about the correspondence, and had secretly carried his letters to and from the mercantile so no one else would know about them. "I'll put it in the outgoing mail sack."

"Maybe you should put it in the outgoing mail sack right now."

"It's safest with the rest of the outgoing mail. That way I don't put it in one sack, then grab another sack, while your letter gets stuck for who knows how long in an extra sack sitting on the shelf."

"That can't possibly happen," he gasped. "Please, say that won't happen. It has to go out tomorrow."

"Mr. Hunter, mail day is day-after-tomorrow. There is no train tomorrow."

He sunk down in a chair. Amanda poured him a cup of coffee and sat in the other chair across from him. "Mr. Hunter, what's wrong? You seem a little mixed-up and confused."

He set his coffee on the table and took off his hat. His hair was a ratty disarray. Amanda noticed the dark circles under his eyes. "I'm a wreck," he admitted. "A complete wreck." He unbuttoned his jacket.

Amanda was shocked to see the change in him. She usually saw him looking at his pocket watch, tapping his toe on the station platform, looking up the track for a train that was more than a minute late or off schedule. He was usually dressed with impeccable tidiness. Now he sat hair uncombed, the buttons on his shirt misbuttoned. "Mr. Hunter, what's wrong?"

"Take good care of that letter for me."

"Do you want to tell me what is so special about this letter?"

"It's my destiny, Amanda. In that letter is a check for train fare. I'm sending it to Mrs. Emma Tate and her two children. She's from Iowa and was widowed two years ago. In that letter, I'm asking her to come to Paradise to be my wife."

Amanda sucked in a breath. "Your wife?"

"I think I'll be a good husband." He added quickly, "And father."

"This is a surprise. Congratulations." Amanda hoped her congratulations didn't sound as hollow as they felt when she'd said the words. *What about love, and being attracted to someone?* Amanda wondered, and said, "I'm happy for you. Tell me about her and the children."

"Mrs. Tate was widowed two years ago when her husband took sick. When her husband died, his brother took over the management of the farm they owned together and was in charge of taking care of her share of it. Last year he lost the farm, along with all of her assets. She has fallen on hard times, and is having a difficult time providing for her children."

"I hope it works out for all of you."

"This is such a lonely place, Amanda, and I'm a lonely man, tired of my own company. I'm going crazy in that depot. I have to be there most of the time to listen for the telegraph all by myself. I need some companionship. I told Mrs. Tate, in my letters, that we have a fine little town here, and while I'm not a rich man, I am comfortable and will provide well for her and the children's needs. I also wrote to her about you and what a good teacher you are and that she needn't worry about the children's education. The two boys are Frank Leslie, who is ten years old, and Christen, who is seven years old.

126

"Mr. Hunter, I will make absolutely sure your letter is in the outgoing mail sack. I hope you will be very, very happy. I'll cancel the stamp right now."

He followed her to the back of the store, saying, "If she accepts my offer, I hope you will have another baseball game and picnic. I would love to come see my own stepchildren, and perhaps in time, my own children, play in a game. It would make me very proud."

"I'm sure we will have lots of baseball games when the weather cooperates." She stamped the cancellation on the envelope. "There, it's ready to go." Amanda slipped it into the outgoing mailbox. "God speed a fast reply."

Mr. Hunter rubbed his mustache and said, "It's all I can do to keep from getting on a horse, riding out of here, and going to Iowa to meet her right this minute. It's going to be hard to wait for an answer." He went to the door and turned, saying, "Good night, Amanda, and thank you."

The next morning's dawn brought rain, sleet, and a dark, dreary day. Amanda went to school early to set the fire in the stove. Her head was full of wonder about Mr. Hunter's new bride-to-be. Amanda had brought an old quilt from home, and for the better part of the school day, she and the students spread it in front of the stove and worked on their lessons there. They kept the stove burning until it was time to go, and Amanda sent the children home in the dreary weather.

When they were gone, she set to work cleaning some of the ashes from the stove with a long-handled scoop and the ash bucket. Jacob Henderson slipped in the door, a book under his arm. Amanda was almost done with the ashes. She said, "Hello, Jacob. I'm almost finished here."

"Let me do that," he offered.

"Nonsense, Jacob, no use in both of us getting soot

on our hands. But if you will, there is a bottle of ink on my desk, some paper on the shelf and a pen in that narrow, middle drawer of my desk.''

Amanda scooped another batch of ashes out of the stove. When she went to dump the scoopfull into the bucket, she remembered that her grade book was on top of the desk, where she had been working on it earlier. She hadn't put it back in the desk drawer on top of Thomas's letters. When Jacob opened the drawer, they would be in plain view. She dropped the scoop in the bucket, spilling ashes as she whirled around in time to see Jacob lift the two envelopes from the drawer.

He studied them. Amanda felt like her heart dropped to her feet, hit the floor hard, then bounced up to the middle of her throat where it stuck in a hard lump. She could barely swallow or breathe, and prayed, *Please, God, don't let him be able to read them.*

But her teaching had been too good, her prayer too late.

He looked at her, eyes full of questions, and said, ''Would you care to explain this?''

Chapter 14

Amanda wrapped her cloak closer about her. The sleet had turned into hard, bird-seed shaped snow that blew in the wind, hitting her face with sharp stings. She sat beside Jacob Henderson on the seat of his wagon. Dread filled her when it creaked and rattled up to the sawmill with its piles of pine logs and pine-scented smoke coming from the chimney. Amanda stepped down, waiting for Jacob to tie off the horses. They opened the sawmill door.

Thomas was pushing a rough log through the big, rotating saw blade. It screamed and sawdust flew as a board peeled away from the log. Jacob motioned to him. Thomas stopped the motor and let the belts slowly chug and squeal to a sickly silence. Amanda wished it wouldn't be so quiet.

"Amanda wants to talk to you," Jacob said.

Thomas looked at her, his eyes full of questions. Amanda didn't know what to say, exactly. She'd had a hard enough time, back at the schoolhouse, explaining it to Jacob when he'd demanded to know what she was doing with the letters.

Jacob insisted they tell Thomas immediately. If ever she felt like a naughty little girl, this was it. Jacob stood close by to make sure she told him the truth. She would much rather have gone to the store, slipped Thomas's letter into his mailbox, and sent Elizabeth's letter on to her. She rued the times she had refused to listen to the good little voice in her head that had told her to do just that.

Now, she clutched the letters in her chilled fingers. "Thomas," she began. "A few weeks ago, a letter came in the mail for you. It was open, and . . ." her voice cracked, she took a deep breath, and continued, her voice wavering. "And I took it, because . . . I . . . was curious." She held the letters forward.

His mouth dropped open as he reached for them. "Why?" was his simple question.

Hot tears made their way down her cold cheeks. "It was wrong, and I'm so sorry. I don't know why I did it, except that I was jealous of her, and I couldn't help myself. I had no right to do it, and if I have interfered with your life, I'm very, very sorry. That last letter you got from her wasn't really from her. I wrote it, then accidentally slipped it in the mail and gave it to you by mistake. No one was supposed to read it. I don't know why I copied her handwriting. I was just . . . just so jealous of her." She hung her head, her face wet with tears. "I hope you will someday forgive me."

He studied the smeared, tattered envelope. "What happened to it?"

"I don't know, it came out of the mail sack like that. I didn't open the letter you wrote to her. I never read it, I just didn't send it to her like I should have to begin with. I've just been keeping it. I don't know why. I'm so very, very sorry."

He pulled the letter from the envelope. Amanda looked to Jacob, who nodded his approval at her apology and put his arm around her. "I'll let you read your letter," she whispered. "If there is anything I can do to fix the damage I've done, or make this up to you, I will." He never said a word, just stared at the page in his hand.

Amanda couldn't stand watching his silence any longer. She stepped out the door and into the wind. Jacob followed her, and said, "Give him a little time. It'll be all right. Hop in the wagon, I'll take you home."

"I'd like to walk, Jacob," she sniffled. "I need some air and I want to be alone."

Amanda walked for a bit, then gathered up her calico skirt and ran as hard as she could down the muddy road. The cold wind whipped against her face and pulled at her cloak, but it didn't compare to the bitterness and chill of Thomas's silence. When she reached the school, her lungs burned and her cheeks were numb. She went inside, knelt in front of the potbellied stove, and tried to warm her hands with the small amount of heat left in the dying fire. She sobbed. After a while, the fire completely died, and the school room was shrouded in cold darkness.

Finally, body aching, she closed the school building and walked toward the mercantile. Not wanting to face anyone, she sneaked up the back staircase to her room to lie on the bed and stare at the ceiling. After a while her father came, holding a lamp. Its light burned her swollen eyes. "Amanda?" he said. "What on earth? I didn't know where you were and was worried about you. Are you ill?" He sat on the edge of the bed and felt her forehead. She grabbed his hand and sobbed. He gathered her in his arms, cradling her, whispering "Shh, it's all right. Shh."

After a few minutes, she was able to tell him everything that had happened. "I understand," she said, her voice hiccuping, "if you don't trust me to handle the mail anymore."

"You've never taken anyone else's mail, have you?"

"Never."

"Why, Amanda, did you take those letters?"

"I was jealous of her. I had a crush on Thomas Lewellen when I was twelve years old, for all the good it did me. I thought, during those two years I was in Omaha, I had gotten over him. When I accepted the teaching job here, I didn't know he would be here, too. When I found out he was, I realized I wasn't over him, that in fact, I love him. Then the letter from Elizabeth came. I couldn't help myself, I took it and forged a letter to Thomas, which I gave to him by accident. I took a second letter, one he wrote to her . . . and now, I've made such a mess. I hate him, father. I hate that I acted like such a dishonest fool. I hate him for loving her and not me." She broke into tears again.

William squeezed her close, and whispered, "I'm so sorry. I would give anything if you didn't have to hurt this way."

"What am I going to do?" she sobbed.

"First, let's clean those tears away." He went to the washstand, poured water from the pitcher into the basin, and wet a washcloth. He carefully wiped her face. The cool water felt good on her hot, sticky skin. "Here," he said, rinsing the cloth again and folding it. "Hold this against your eyes for a while." She did as he instructed. He took her hairbrush from the dresser and began brushing the tangles and wind-rats from her hair. "It's been a long time since I brushed my little girl's hair for her," he said, a teasing tone in his voice.

"I'm sorry," Amanda said, her voice stronger, "if I betrayed your trust in me."

"You did nothing of the kind. It wasn't right, but I understand. It would be my wish that it doesn't happen again, but I can completely forgive."

One more tear squeezed its way out of the corner of

her eye. "Thank you. It won't ever happen again. I feel like such a fool."

"Love makes us all feel that way, at one time or another."

"Did you ever feel like a fool with Mama?"

"From the day I met her, until the day she said, 'I do,' and married me."

"You did? Really? Do you think you'll ever marry again?"

"I doubt it. I loved your mother very much, and I loved being married, but I don't have the courage and fortitude to go through what you are going through right now. "

Amanda laughed. "I can understand why, unless you do it like . . . like . . . oh dear, I promised I wouldn't tell."

"Don't break your promise unless it's something I should know about."

"I'm not sure if it is or not. I've been hand-delivering Mr. Hunter's mail because he doesn't want anyone to know he's getting letters from someone special. The other night, he brought a letter in to me, and he said . . . promise you won't tell?"

"I promise."

"He said he was asking her to marry him. See how simple it was for him?"

"Then why is Mr. Hunter sneaking around, having you hand-deliver his mail?"

Amanda thought about it and remembered his tattered appearance and the tight worry lines on his face when he'd brought her the last letter. "On second thought, you're right, Father. I don't think it's easy for anyone."

"I rest my case." He set her brush on the dresser. "Do you want something to eat?"

"No, thank you. I couldn't. My stomach is full of butterflies."

"Get ready for bed. I'll see what we have on the shelves downstairs for butterflies in the stomach."

Amanda dressed in her nightgown and hung her skirt and cloak in the armoire. Her father tapped on the door just as she snuggled into bed. He carried a bottle and a spoon. "Here we go, Dr. Bertram's elixir." He read the bottle label. "It doesn't say anything about broken hearts, butterflies in the stomach, and the aftereffects of foolish actions. It does, however, work on other symptoms like excitable stomach, depressions, vapors, and sleeplessness." He poured her a big spoonful and tipped it into her open mouth. The bitter taste made her shudder. It burned all the way down to her stomach, made her lungs tingle, and cleared her sinuses in one fiery surge. "Phew, that's strong stuff."

William tucked the quilts around her. She snuggled down into the comfort of her bed. "Are you warm enough?" he asked, bending his angular frame over her. "Do you want me to go first thing in the morning and cancel school?"

"I'll see how I feel tomorrow. No use making the children suffer, too, because of my foolishness."

He pulled the chair up close to the bed, sat, and took her hand. "Amanda, I'm sorry Thomas can't see what I see when I look at you. You are a beautiful, hardworking, sweet young woman. Any man would be proud to have you love him and be his wife. Give it time, and you'll find that somewhere, there is someone who will be everything you want and need. Be patient, true love will come in its own sweet time."

Amanda's head felt woozy. Her eyes grew heavy. The elixir gave her a floating, sleepy feeling. She squeezed her father's hand. "I love you," she whispered, and fell asleep.

When she woke in the morning, her head felt heavy and her eyes still stung. She dressed in a lace-trimmed calico dress and went out to the kitchen. Her father poured her a glass of milk and sliced pieces of cheddar cheese and bread for her.

Amanda drank the milk and nibbled at the cheese. Looking out the window, she saw that a heavy frost had coated every surface, giving the town a fairy-tale, crystal appearance. "Brr," Amanda shivered. "I better go start a fire at the school so it won't be so cold when the children come. I'll see you this afternoon."

Amanda found that when she focused on the children and their lessons, she could forget about Thomas. She felt a deep sense of relief whenever she opened her middle desk drawer and the letters were gone. *That's one thing you have to say for the act of confessing,* she thought. *It cleanses the soul of guilt.* By the time school was over for the day and the children were gathering their gloves, coats, and lunch pails, Amanda felt more lighthearted and teased and hugged the children as they left the building. She banked the fire in the stove, then pulled her own cloak around herself and left the school. At the mercantile, she grabbed the outgoing mail sack, checking to make sure Mr. Hunter's letter was safely nestled inside with the others. "Please return a happy answer," she told the envelope, then tightened the sack strings and knotted them.

At the train station, Mr. Hunter stood and watched her coming down the street. "It's in there, isn't it?" he asked when she handed the sack to him.

"I double-checked."

"Good. Will you hand it to the conductor? I'm going to be sick." He ran around the side of the building. Amanda stood next to the train and waited for the conductor to walk up the grade. "Mr. Hunter isn't feeling well today," she told him, and handed him the sack.

"I thought he looked a little bit peeked when we

were unloading the freight," the uniformed conductor said, taking the sack. "Tell him to take care and eat some chicken soup. It'll make him feel better real quick."

The train pulled out of the station, and Amanda went into the depot. Mr. Hunter was coming down the stairs, wiping his face with a towel. The hair around his face was damp. "Are you okay, Mr. Hunter?"

"I'm fine." He chuckled, "Just had to wash my face. Who would have thought I would get so tied up in knots over a silly letter."

"Believe me, Mr. Hunter, I am the one person in this world who completely understands." Her voice was full of genuine sympathy. "It's on its way now. It won't be long, and you'll know something. I'll keep my fingers crossed for good news to come your way."

"Thank you, Amanda. I wouldn't have had the guts to do this if you hadn't been here to help me." He handed her the incoming mail sack.

"I really didn't do that much. Um . . . Mr. Hunter, if you find yourself having trouble sleeping and your stomach is upset, my father has some elixir up at the mercantile that really helps. Would you like me to wrap up a bottle of it for you?"

"That would be nice. Thank you. I'll come get it later."

Amanda carried the mail sack to the mercantile. There was a letter to her from Laura. She quietly set it aside, keeping it a secret on purpose, because she didn't feel like sharing it or talking too much. The men gathered around the stove were pouring cups of coffee and arguing over the headlines of the paper. The debate turned to the issue of women having the right to vote, and a lively discussion began until Jacob Henderson walked into the store. The voices went quiet.

Jacob said, "What were you talking about?" No one

said anything. "I imagine it was about women having the right to vote?" Jacob answered his own question, then went and stood directly in front of the livery-barn owner, Cal Taneman. "Cal, I'm sorry that the last time we met in here, I let my arguments force you into punching me in the mouth. I don't think that particular argument warranted my getting punched in the mouth . . ." The room went deadly silent. Amanda's eyes widened. "But other things I've said to you about your roof and other things in the past certainly did warrant my being punched in the mouth, long before that. I'm truly sorry that I haven't been a better neighbor. That's a fine livery barn you put up over there and it will serve you well for many years to come. I wish you and your business much success."

Jacob held out his hand. Cal scratched his bushy head and slowly took the offered hand. "Thank you for saying so, Jacob. I'm sorry I let my temper get the best of me. I shouldn't have hit you. I hope you'll forgive me. If my roof ever sags, I'll call on you to help me fix it. Can I pour you a cup of coffee?"

"No, thank you. But next time I'm in, I'll drink a cup with you. I need to get my mail and talk to Amanda for a moment, then I best get back to the sawmill. Next mail day, we'll share a cup of coffee . . ." He looked at Amanda out of the corner of his eye and winked, a proud smile covering his face. "And we'll *read* the paper and share opinions about the articles in it. I'm sure we'll disagree on most things, and it will be just grand, my friend." They both laughed, and the crowd joined them. They shook hands again and Jacob made his way to Amanda at the back counter. "I need to have a word with you in private," he whispered.

Amanda led the way to the back room. She pulled a crate forward and sat on it. He pulled up a crate and sat, too. Amanda felt a little uncomfortable, and was still a little angry at him for forcing her to apologize to Thomas for what she had done, even though she knew it was the right thing to do.

"Apologizing is hard, isn't it?" Jacob said. "When someone else forces you to do it, or you force yourself. It's not in the least bit enjoyable, but it does feel good when you finally do," he said, nudging her, trying to make her smile. "I will never say another word about Cal Taneman's roof again. If it needs fixing later, it can be fixed. But hard feelings are very difficult to try to fix later. Are you still angry with me?"

Amanda's tongue stumbled over the words, "A little. But you're right, it feels good to have those letters off my conscience. Apologizing didn't feel good at the time, and to tell the truth, it still doesn't."

"I'm very sorry for what I did to you. At the time, making you apologize seemed like the right thing to do, but now I don't think so, for several reasons. You were very brave, yesterday, to admit to Thomas that you made a mistake. It made me realize that my fight with Cal Taneman was causing an uncomfortable split in our little town. The longer I put off apologizing to him, the harder it would be to fix things. So I decided to make my peace with him before he wouldn't forgive me and we wouldn't be able to mend our problems. And now, this is hard to say, but I wanted to be the one to tell you. Thomas is gone."

"Gone?"

"He came to the sawmill early this morning and said he was sorry, but he had some business to take care of in Texas, something he said he'd put off for far too long. He asked me to take care of his house until he returns. He didn't know how long it would be. I'm so sorry, Amanda. My rash and seemingly righteous behavior yesterday caused me to lose my best sawmill partner, and you to lose your true love. We should have just slipped those letters into the mail and kept quiet."

Amanda fought back the tears. "Jacob," she said in a measured voice, "you were right. I did wrong, and I owed him an apology. But he isn't my true love, he doesn't love me. I can accept that now, and I'm ready to get on with my life. Someday, maybe, I will love another special person who will return my love. But that special person isn't Thomas."

"When you were a little girl, you followed him around like a little pup. Do you remember telling me and Claire that someday you were going to grow up and marry him?"

"I was a child then. Now that I have grown up, I realize Thomas doesn't follow me around like a little puppy. He doesn't spend every spare moment thinking about me. To be true love, Jacob, it has to go both ways. I could love him till the cows come home, and it won't do me a bit of good. Don't you see that, Jacob?"

"Don't give up on him, yet."

"Do you want me to stay around here and get my hopes up waiting for him? What happens when he comes back from Texas with a new bride at his side? What then, Jacob? There isn't enough elixir on the shelves of this store to heal how I would feel then. As far as I'm concerned, Thomas Lewellen can stay in Texas. I'm sorry about your business partner and all, but I never want to see him again."

Chapter 15

Amanda felt numb for several days. Whenever she started to think about Thomas, she forced herself to stop and threw herself into her work: polishing the floors at school and rearranging merchandise at the mercantile. She and Jacob helped her father build shelves for the new root cellar. Then, like the sun clearing away the clouds after a storm, she started to feel better.

When the root cellar was finished, Amanda helped move some of the inventory onto its shelves. From the upstairs storeroom, they moved the stock that couldn't be frozen or that needed to stay cool. William showed all the customers the new cellar, saying, "Now we'll be able to keep eggs and milk cool in the summer and protect them from freezing in the winter. We'll be able to get a little produce every now and then. Just think, we'll be able to get bananas and oranges at Christmas and keep them longer. Won't it be nice."

One day, as Amanda, her father, and Jacob Henderson were standing outside the root cellar talking, Mr. Hunter came running and yelling, "Amanda, Amanda! Look! Look at this telegram!"

Amanda took the piece of paper from him. It said,

Accepting your offer. Arriving Nov. 3, to be your bride. Have preacher at train station. Emma Tate.

"She said yes!" Amanda rejoiced. "Mr. Hunter, I'm so happy for you. What can I do to help you get ready for her?"

"Huh? Get ready?" He seemed truly astounded.

"For the wedding, and for your new family."

"I guess I never thought about any of that. I just told her we could get married as soon as she got here. I guess that's okay with her. It's okay with me, I'm getting married. I need to get a preacher from Cheyenne to come marry us, and cake, and . . ."

Jacob clapped Mr. Hunter on the shoulder and congratulated him. "What do you need us to do?" he asked. "We should do something special for the very first wedding in Paradise."

"I don't rightly know, Jacob, I've never been married before. Amanda, I'd be right proud and grateful if you'd help me take care of the details."

"I'd be happy to, Mr. Hunter."

The next few days passed quickly as Amanda busied herself with a flurry of wedding arrangements. She declared November 3 a holiday from school so all the children, as well as she, could attend the wedding. Everyone in town was invited to come to the ceremony at the train station. Mrs. McClain offered to bake a cake. Amanda and Claire Henderson cleaned and polished the station house from top to bottom. The woodwork gleamed and the clean, mellow smell of furniture oil permeated the station house. Mr. Hunter arranged for a circuit preacher to come from Cheyenne. At school, Amanda's students cut and painted paper flowers to decorate the station. Amanda wished it was summer so they could gather wild irises from the banks of the creek. "Oh well," she sighed, as she surveyed her students' handiwork. "We'll do the best we can and hope she feels welcome." She had a niggling sense of apprehension. Wouldn't Emma Tate want to see her fiancé and get to know him first before they got married? Wouldn't she want to see if she liked him, let alone loved him? Could she possibly know she loved him just from his letters? Amanda shuddered and thought, *It's too daring for me.*

On the big day, the cantankerous Wyoming weather cooperated, and was unseasonably warm and mellow. The wind didn't blow a whit. Amanda was grateful for the nice day as she dressed in her best lace dress and arranged her auburn hair on top of her head.

By early afternoon, she stood at the station house greeting guests as they came carrying gifts for the couple. She guessed that everyone in town, with the exception of Thomas, of course, had come to the wedding. They all stood visiting and anxiously waiting for the train that would bring Mr. Hunter's bride and new family. Mr. Hunter stood on the platform and watched the tracks, trying to get a glimpse of the train. Amanda stepped outside to wait with him. He fretted, "What if the train doesn't come? What if she missed it? What if she changed her mind?"

"Mr. Hunter, what can go wrong? The station looks grand, the cake and punch are on the table. The preacher is here. All we need is the bride." She reached up and tucked one of his unruly strands of hair into place.

He stewed, "I'm scared, Amanda. What if she finds she can't come to love me after all? What if she doesn't like it here in Paradise?"

Amanda tried to reassure him. "Trust yourself. You liked her letters, didn't you? If she gets off the train and you have any doubts, you can wait, or get her a train ticket to go back home. It won't hurt anything."

Far down the track, they could hear the train whistle blow.

"Here it comes," Amanda said, "Relax, Mr. Hunter." She straightened his tie for him.

As the train approached, the guests poured out of the station house onto the platform to see the bride. Amanda's father and Cal Taneman stood ready to take over Mr. Hunter's duties receiving the mail so that Mr. Hunter could greet his bride.

The train slowed to a stop. A short, pert, brown-haired woman with two young boys stepped from the passenger car. She was dressed in a smart, dark-green, wool traveling suit and a matching hat. The boys were dressed in Sunday-best suits and ties. She had a gentle but anxious look on her face. Mr. Hunter stepped forward and helped her and the children step from the train. "Are you Emma Tate?" he asked.

"Robert Hunter? So nice to meet you. These are my children, Frank and Christen."

"I'm glad to meet you, Frank and Christen. I hope you will be happy here." He beamed at his bride. Slowly, shyly, she smiled back. "Ladies and gentlemen," he proclaimed, "I'd like you to meet my bride, Emma Tate." Everyone on the platform applauded. Amanda went to Emma's side and whispered, "I have a room upstairs ready for you, if you'd like to freshen up before the ceremony."

"That would be very nice," she said, trying to say hello to everyone Mr. Hunter introduced her to as they made their way through the crowd and into the station house.

Amanda led the way upstairs to one of the bedrooms, where she said, "It's very nice to meet you, Mrs. Tate. If there is anything you need, just ask. I'm Amanda Chappell."

"Oh, of course. Amanda Chappell. You're the

teacher. Mr. Hunter wrote so many wonderful things about you in his letters." Emma had a musical voice and a gracious manner.

"That was kind of him." Amanda felt herself blush at the compliment. "I hope your children will like our school."

Emma took off her hat and adjusted her hair and suit. "Tell me something, Amanda, and do be honest. Is Mr. Hunter a kind man?"

"I think he's a very nice man. He's quiet, tidy, punctual, and looking forward to being a father."

Emma sighed with relief. "That's good to know. I'm a nervous wreck."

Amanda took her hands and squeezed them. "Do you want to wait for a few days, and get to know him better? I'm sure he won't mind. You can stay with my father and me."

"No, it's quite all right. I'm sure you know my situation. It's quite desperate. My husband left me with some property, but his brother was given charge of it. He lost it, and now I have no money, and I'm not properly trained for any kind of employment, except to be a homemaker and a mother. If I could get a job, I have no one to care for my boys." She wiped a tear from the edge of her eye. "We used the last bit of food we had to make a lunch to last us on the trip out here. It was the last of the groceries I had in the house, and we had no money to buy meals while we traveled. I don't have any other choices, Amanda. So you see, I do want very much for this to work, not just for me, but for my two boys."

Amanda didn't know how to tell Emma that her experience, so far, had been that life had no guarantees. But she knew that Emma probably knew that better than anyone else, and said, "I hope that you will like it in

Paradise, and that you will be very happy. I will do everything I can to help you. I have a present for you.''

Amanda took a wrapped hatbox from the dresser and handed it to her. "I'm sorry we don't have fresh flowers for you on your wedding day, but maybe this will work instead. Claire Henderson and I made it. You'll meet Claire later.''

She unwrapped the box, gasped, and took out a bouquet of flowers made from bright satin ribbons and white lace. "How beautiful," she exclaimed, and started to cry. "I don't remember the last time anyone did such a lovely and nice thing for me. Thank you very much. It's so pretty." Amanda helped wipe her tears with a lace handkerchief. "I think I'm going to like it here," Emma said, and wiped away the last tear, looked in the mirror one more time to straighten her hair and shoulders, took the bouquet, and said, "I'm ready."

The crowd hushed when Amanda and Emma stood at the top of the stairs and then descended. Mr. Hunter and her two boys waited at the bottom, looking up at them.

Mr. Hunter offered his hand. Emma took it, and they approached the preacher, who opened his Bible and began reading. Amanda watched as the couple stood holding hands, repeating their wedding vows. Mr. Hunter looked into Emma's eyes. She reluctantly looked up into his. Their eyes met, they stared at each other, and it seemed for a moment that they were the only two people on earth. Amanda sighed and wiped a tear from her eye when the preacher pronounced them man and wife. The crowd clapped and cheered as Mr. Hunter placed an affectionate kiss on her cheek.

When the ceremony ended, the crowd stayed for a long time, visiting, eating cake, having punch, and getting acquainted with the new Mrs. Hunter. Emma's two children, Frank and Christen, quickly got acquainted with the other children, and all of them were running, laughing, and playing tag like they had known each other forever. With a kind but no-nonsense suggestion, Claire sent all of them outside to play. They each grabbed some cake and ran outside with a peal of laughter. Their gay mood matched the joy of the adult guests at the wedding.

Finally, the party wound down, and all of the guests left. Amanda and Claire helped clean the depot, wash the dishes, and pick up the decorations before they bid the new couple good-bye.

They walked to the mercantile, where Jacob, her father, and several other people were gathered. They all stared at Amanda when she walked into the store. Amanda got the uncomfortable feeling that she had been the topic of their conversation. "What?" she asked, feeling self-conscious. "Amanda," said Jacob. "That was a beautiful wedding. We very much like Mr. Hunter's new bride, and we are going to do everything we can to make her feel welcome and to help her adjust to her new life here. We've been talking about her and you and several things." Jacob put his arm around Claire. "We think what happened to Mrs. Tate's, I mean the new Mrs. Hunter's, farm land is a real shame. It sure wasn't right that she lost all her property. While we are glad she's here with us and married to Mr. Hunter, we just don't like the circumstances that made her have to be here, marrying a man she doesn't know in order to care for her children."

Cal Taneman said, "We're all just working hard to have something nice for our children."

"If something happens to one of us," Jacob said, "the way the laws are written, our wives won't be able to keep the things we have worked so hard for. To make a long story short, Amanda, you were right, and we're all here to tell you that."

"I was right about what?"

"Women getting the right to vote," Jacob explained.

Amanda couldn't believe her ears. "What are you saying?"

Jacob gave her a broad smile. "It was your interest and passion for this issue that made all of us open our eyes and pay attention in the first place. Maybe, just maybe, giving women the right to vote will be the first step in helping our families protect themselves and our property, in case something happens to us, and we aren't here to look after them."

"We've talked it over," Cal Taneman said. "Tomorrow, Jacob is going to go to Cheyenne to have a talk with Colonel Bright, the legislator from South Pass City who promised to introduce a bill for women's suffrage. Jacob is going to tell him that here in Paradise, we support giving women the right to vote."

"Jacob!" Amanda threw her arms around him and gave him a squeeze. "Do you really mean it?"

"On my honor," said Jacob. "I'll be leaving at daylight, so I best get home, do my chores, and get some sleep so I'll be ready to ride at dawn. Good-bye, everyone."

Amanda walked out on the boardwalk with Jacob and Claire. "Jacob, what changed your mind so drastically?"

"You did, Amanda. I think you know why," he said, winking. "I've reconsidered my position. One of the reasons is that I think it's high time intelligent women like you and Claire have the right to vote. Wish me luck in Cheyenne."

That night, Amanda tossed and turned in her bed. She whispered a prayer, "Please, God, help Jacob speak well for us. Please, let him make a difference, and most of all, please don't let someone punch him in the nose."

At dawn, Amanda heard a horse moving in the street below her window. She hustled out of bed and stood at the window. Jacob rode by, heading east. He looked up at her window, noticed her standing there, and waved. Amanda waved to him and watched him ride out of town until his horse disappeared. "God speed your way," she whispered, blowing him a kiss for luck.

Chapter 16

Later that morning, Amanda arrived at school feeling as prickly as a pincushion. She tried to visualize where Jacob would be on his journey to Cheyenne. She didn't know if she could wait to hear from him. She stepped out on the steps of the school with the broom, and swept the dirt and dried leaves from the steps. The new couple, Mr. and Mrs. Hunter, walked up the street toward the school. They were holding hands, their faces bright, and making lively conversation. The two boys kicked an empty tin can up the street, chasing it and laughing. Their laughter floated up the street on the cool breeze. Amanda leaned on her broom and sighed. She noticed the way the new couple looked at each other and knew, that somewhere between a postage stamp on an envelope to a lonely hearts club and this bright, chilly morning, love had blossomed. *Is it really that easy?* she asked herself. *If it is, maybe it can happen for me.* Once again, she felt the sting of Thomas's rejection, but brushed the feelings aside as the Hunter family stepped into the schoolyard.

"Welcome to our school," Amanda called, giving them a bright smile. "Hello, Frank and Christen."

"Are we going to play baseball?" Christen asked.

"Mr. Hunter . . . I mean . . . my new papa and the other kids at the wedding said we get to play baseball at this school."

Amanda looked at Mr. Hunter. He beamed with pride. "We play when the weather is good. It's so fickle right now, cold and snowy one day, and sunny the next. If you can be patient and wait for the right weather, I promise we'll play more baseball than you can stand. Let's put your lunch pails in the cloakroom and assign each of you a seat."

They went inside the building. "I'm so glad they're going to be in our school," Amanda told Mrs. Hunter. "We'll do everything we can to make them feel welcome."

"You already have," Emma said. "Thank you for the beautiful wedding yesterday. The children made some new friends there, and we feel like we belong already. I'm going to like Paradise very much, and I hope to make Mr. Hunter as happy as he's made me." She took his hand and smiled up at him. He seemed to glow in the light of her smile.

Amanda assigned the boys each a seat and entered their names in the grade ledger. The other students arrived, and they all ran outside to play for a few minutes before school started. Mr. and Mrs. Hunter took their leave, and walked down the street holding hands.

The two new boys blended in well with the other children. Amanda assigned each of them to a baseball team, even though it was too chilly to play. By the time the day ended, it seemed as if they had always been in the Paradise school. After school, they left with the other children, laughing and playing. Amanda was happy with her new students, and in the calm, after the children left, she missed her old student, Jacob. She thought about him and wondered if he had reached Cheyenne. *Has he had a chance to talk to Colonel*

Bright? She missed their lively reading lessons and knew that soon, he would no longer need her. His reading skills had improved so fast and so well. She cleaned the blackboards, finished her work for the day, pulled her shawl about her, and went home.

Amanda could hardly stand waiting to hear something, anything, from Jacob as she donned an apron and helped in the mercantile. She was cutting a length of calico cloth from a thick bolt for Mrs. Taneman when Mr. Hunter rushed into the store.

"Look, Amanda, a telegram for you," he shouted.

She dropped the scissors and grabbed the telegram. It said, *Bright will introduce bill. Be home soon, Jacob.* Her heart thumped with excitement when she read the words. "He did it," Amanda shouted. He must have talked to Colonel Bright. Amanda showed the telegram to anyone and everyone who came into the store, her heart beating a little faster every time she did. She read it so many times, her eyes hurt. "It says something, but so little," Amanda remarked to her father. "Don't you hate telegrams? They cost so much to send, you almost can't say anything when you do."

William laughed at her frustrations and said, "Dear daughter, we'll have to wait for Jacob to get back so we can find out more."

"I can't stand it until he gets back."

The next morning came with wet flakes of snow falling so thick Amanda could hardly see across the street. "Oh, no," she howled and ran, barefoot, still in her nightgown, to the kitchen where her father was grinding coffee beans. "Tell me the snow won't keep Jacob from coming home today," she begged

William laughed. "Jacob is a hardy cuss. He'll be home today. Count on him."

"I can't wait to talk to him and hear what he has to say."

Amanda had to make herself get ready for school and walk up the street to the school. Off and on during the morning, she looked out the tall windows and looked for Jacob and his bay horse. At noon, heavy snow covered the ground. Amanda and the children sat on the quilt by the potbellied stove to eat their lunches. The children watched the snow falling outside the windows and seemed to sense her apprehensive mood. She told them, "I'm anxious about Jacob Henderson. He went to Cheyenne, our territorial capital. The very first Wyoming Territorial Legislature is meeting now. Remember when we talked about that election back in September? The people who were elected then are now voting on the new laws we will have. Jacob went to talk to some of the representatives about some of the laws we think are important. He asked one of the representatives to introduce a bill so the legislature can vote for it."

"Is that the women's suffrage bill?" Marie McClain asked.

"Yes," Amanda answered. "Isn't it exciting? Jacob talked to a man from South Pass City who promised to introduce the bill. Now, I'm on pins and needles waiting for him to come home and tell us what happened while he was there."

"I hope they vote on the law," Carrie Taneman said. "Because when I grow up, I want to vote."

Amanda felt uncomfortable talking about political matters with the children, and didn't want to take the risk of making someone mad again. She changed the subject. "Children, we have something we're going to need to talk about. The weather is going to keep getting worse as we get deeper into winter. I fully expect the snow today will melt off. But soon, it'll pile up and will be here to stay. The days are getting darker earlier and earlier. Soon, we won't be able to see inside our school building without lamps. That won't be good. We will need to close school during the darkest, cold winter months.''

"No! Don't do that! Please, don't," the children begged.

"It's for the best," said Amanda. "Then we won't have to worry about you walking to school in a terrible snowstorm or something. Let me tell you what I was thinking. If we close at the middle of December, we could have a big Christmas party and invite our parents, and everyone else who wants to come. We could put on a play for them or something."

The children's eyes brightened at the idea. "Would we all be in the play?" Willy Taneman asked.

"Everyone will be in the play," Amanda promised. "Then we'll end school for a couple of months. We'll come back in early March. By then, we'll have more daylight and some nice spring weather. Guess what we can do again?''

"Baseball!" the children shouted.

For the rest of the day, the children's bubbling excitement over the prospect of nice weather and the return of baseball helped lift Amanda's worried spirits. After school, she looked out the window and saw a lone bay horse tied to the hitching post in front of the mercantile. Amanda grabbed her cloak and ran all the way to the store.

"Jacob," she cried, running into the mercantile. "Jacob, tell us about your trip!"

"I just walked in and barely took my coat off. I'll take a cup of that hot coffee," he said, shivering.

Amanda couldn't stand it. She poured him a cup of coffee and handed it to him. He seemed to take forever, warming his hands, sipping his coffee. She wanted to grab his shoulders and yell, "talk, mister!" People flocked into the store as the word spread that Jacob was back. Amanda figured he was waiting for the maximum crowd to gather. She thought, *Go ahead, talk, you can always tell it again.*

Finally, when the store was full of people, he settled in a chair by the stove and took a sip of coffee. "I'm happy to report," he said, "that I met Colonel Bright. I had two chances to talk to him. Yesterday, early afternoon before I sent the telegram, I talked to him. Then last night I saw him at the hotel, bought him a drink, and we talked some more. I told him how we feel here in Paradise, and he feels the same way we do. I also told him about our fine teacher, Miss Amanda . . ."

Amanda felt herself blush.

"He listened to everything I had to say."

"What was he like?" William asked.

"A very nice, considerate, genteel man. He has a very well-educated and accomplished young wife. He says the bill will face some terrible opposition and expects that the worse of it will come from another South Pass City legislator, Mr. Ben Sheeks."

Amanda held her breath. Opposition or not, they had a promise that the bill would at least be introduced. A promise was better than nothing; a promise was the seed of hope. Jacob answered more questions and repeated his tale for the newcomers that straggled into the store late. Finally he stood, bundled his coat around him, and went home to his family and chores. Amanda finished the day and the weekend with happy thoughts tumbling through her mind.

On Monday afternoon, Amanda hurried home from school to take care of the mail. When she sorted the incoming mail, there were two letters addressed to her, one from Laura and one from Thomas. Amanda didn't feel like sharing them with everyone else, and hid them in her pocket until she could get a private moment to read them by herself.

That night after supper, her first moment alone, she settled herself on a stool at the counter in the soft glow of a lamp with pen, ink, and stationery before her. She tore open Thomas's letter, her hands shaking.

Dear Amanda,
I'm sorry I left so fast and didn't have a chance to talk to you. We need to talk and will when I return. I'm not for sure when that will be, but I hope soon.

Ever yours, Thomas.

Amanda read the letter again, not understanding. "Are you coming alone, or with a southern belle on your arm?" she questioned aloud. "What happened, Thomas? Did she reject you, after all? Is that why you're coming home?"

Amanda heard her father coming down the steps. She quickly stuffed Thomas's letter into her pocket, and tore open Laura's letter. It was short, sweet, and simple.

Dear Amanda,
I've had a busy, busy time here. I need to ask you to release me from our promise never to marry. I've met someone. He is so wonderful, nothing else seems to matter to me at the moment. Surely you will understand. I've never been happier. I'll write more when I can.

Love, Laura.

William stepped into the room as Amanda brushed a tear from her cheek. "Hey, what's the matter?"

Amanda handed him Laura's letter and snuggled into

the arm he put around her shoulders. He finished reading and asked, "What made you so sad?"

"I'm just jealous that she found someone and I have no one."

"I'm so sorry, sweetheart. Someday it will happen for you, too."

"I know it will. It just hit me wrong because we were going to change the world and make a difference."

"Amanda, every day you go into that school, you make a difference. You are the reason Jacob went to Cheyenne, and who knows what will happen as a result of that."

"I know. You're right. Those tears were as much happy ones for her as anything else. I'm going to write back to her, and tell her how happy I am for her."

"You sure you're all right?"

"I'm fine."

"I'm going to work on some books for a few minutes."

He went to his desk and shuffled through some papers as Amanda took a pen in hand and wrote a note to Laura releasing her from the pact they had made so long ago on the train when they had first met. Amanda told her all about school, and that Colonel Bright promised Jacob he would introduce the suffrage bill. She finished the letter saying, *I am very happy for you and your good news. I hope you will be very happy and wish you all the very best with your new beau.* She paused and thought about what she was writing. In some ways, she felt a little betrayed. It was hard to be sincerely happy for her friend and for Mr. Hunter and his new bride when she had to fight back the jealous pangs that welled up inside her. Her heart ached when she thought about Thomas's letter in her pocket. She wrote, *Laura, I've given it some thought. I don't know that we need to sacrifice our lives and happiness for the cause of equality for women. I know, I don't want to go to war to win our equality. I have . . .* Amanda thought about Thomas and didn't know if she wanted to use the word friend or not. She wrote, *an acquaintance who fought in the war between the states. When I remember that terrible war, and the loss of property and lives, it makes me think, I don't want the right to vote and equality if the price of those privileges is one, single human life. The price is too high for me. I am willing to take the battle for equality slower and more peacefully, even if it takes longer than my lifetime. We can effect change, eventually. I know in my heart that women will one day be equal. As teachers, we have in our power the ability to try to educate those around us about our cause. If we do that, someday we will win the long, slow battle. So plan your life, be happy, and don't give up hope that we will one day be equal to men. Love, Amanda.*

As Amanda finished her letter, her father took a stack of papers, kissed her on top of the head, and said, "Good night. Don't stay up too late."

"I won't." As the sound of his footsteps disappeared up the steps, Amanda forced herself to face the truth, and admitted to herself that she was jealous of Laura. What she really wanted was to fall in love, to be in love, and to experience true love. "It is never going to happen to me here in Paradise," Amanda said. "Never." She pulled Thomas's letter from her pocket. "You are never going to love me, and I can accept that. But I won't make myself get on with my life as long as I'm around you and constantly reminded of the feelings I have for you. I'm moving on, no matter what it takes to get that done. And if she rejected you, are you now interested in me? Forget it."

She went to the stove, opened the door, and started

to throw Thomas's letter into the fire. Something stayed her hand and made her read it again.

Dear Amanda,
I'm sorry I left so fast and didn't have a chance to talk to you. We need to talk and will when I return. I'm not for sure when that will be, but I hope soon.

Ever yours, Thomas.

"So why didn't you send a telegram, Thomas? No more than this letter says, you might as well have not written. Are we just friends? Does she or doesn't she love you? What aren't you telling me? What did she do, choose him and not you? Now that she's marrying someone else, you want me? What am I, your second fiddle? Her leftovers?" She threw the letter into the fire, watched it burn, and slammed the door shut. "I won't be anyone's second choice, Thomas. Especially not yours."

Chapter 17

After school on November 12, Amanda sat at her desk grading the slates when Mr. Hunter burst into the schoolroom shouting, "It happened! Colonel Bright publicly announced that he *will* introduce a suffrage bill. We just got word over the telegraph wire."

"What?" Amanda jumped from her seat and grabbed the telegram out of his hand. "He will? He'll do it?" Tears filled her eyes. "I had given up hope that it would ever happen." She wiped her eyes and laughed. "Does everyone else know?"

"You're the first one I told. Should we tell the others?"

Amanda grabbed Mr. Hunter around his generous middle. They hurried toward the mercantile to share the good news. Everyone in the store applauded at the announcement. Jacob Henderson said, "He's as good as his promise." He raised his coffee cup. "Here's to the bill and its safe journey and passage." Amanda wondered how long it would be before they heard more.

The wind blustered and blew into Thanksgiving. Amanda still watched and waited for word on the bill. For one long day after another, there was no news. When Thanksgiving came, Amanda, her father, and the

Hunter family went to the Hendersons' house for Thanksgiving dinner. Claire served a roasted wild turkey with corn-bread stuffing; stewed apples; mashed potatoes made with thick cream; gravy; and sweet potatoes glazed with molasses. After dinner, Amanda, Claire, and Emma talked companionably as they washed the dishes, then joined the men in the sitting room. The children invited Amanda to go sledding with them, but she declined and sat by her father.

After the children ran outside to play, Amanda said, "I wanted all of you to know," she began, "my father and I have discussed this, and at the end of the school year, I'm resigning from my teaching position and accepting a job somewhere else. I wanted to tell you now, so you can make plans to look for a new teacher. Please don't tell the children yet. I'll do it when the time is right."

Silence met her announcement.

"What on earth are you talking about?" Claire asked, breaking the quiet.

"This isn't easy for me," Amanda admitted. "But I think it's best. I need to go someplace where I have more social opportunities and a chance to meet other people my age."

"I wish you would reconsider," Emma Hunter said, "my boys love school, and they have never liked it before now. I know it's because of you."

Jacob studied her. It was his reaction that she dreaded the most. They had no fear of being honest with each other. His silence scared her. He finally said, "Amanda, let's go in the kitchen and get a piece of pie."

Amanda followed him into the kitchen. He picked up a knife and sliced into a pumpkin pie with swift, ferocious movements. "Why?"

"I need to move on, Jacob. I think it's for the best."

"It's Thomas, isn't it?"

"Jacob, please don't make this hard for me. Do you know how painful this has been for me? I wanted to curl up and die when I first came here and found out he was here, too. I told myself I could handle being around him. But I was wrong. The more time I spend around him, the more I love him. I can't do it any longer, Jacob. I can't be in this small community, feeling the way I do, knowing he doesn't feel the same way about me. I'm going where he isn't. I love my students, I love Paradise, I love being with all of you, but it's too hard. Jacob, try to understand."

He threw the knife on the table with a clatter. "I understand," he said, his voice angry. "But that doesn't mean I have to like it. All of a sudden, I don't feel like having pie." He grabbed her in an intense hug and said, "I want you to be happy, even at the expense of our losing you. No one in Paradise wants you to go."

They rejoined the rest of the group and William said, "It's getting late, we'd better go, Amanda."

Amanda knew her announcement had put a damper on everyone's enjoyment of the holiday, and felt terrible for ruining the good time.

A blue, dreary mood surrounded Amanda, until a few days later, on November 27, when Mr. Hunter came bursting into the schoolroom bubbling with excitement. "He did it, Amanda. He did it. The telegraph wires are singing with the news. Today Colonel Bright introduced the women's suffrage bill, giving women the right to vote at age eighteen. It's introduced."

Amanda grabbed him and shouted with excitement. Her students joined the celebrating and yelled, "Yippee, hooray, Amanda! He did it!"

Amanda bubbled, "Everyone get your things. School is out for the day. Let's go down to the mercantile. I bet Mr. Chappell will want to help us celebrate with sugar sticks."

161

The children's voices raised in another shout of celebration, "Candy! Hooray, for candy!"

They hurried and gathered their belongings and rushed down to the mercantile, where the children's parents were gathering. "Did you hear?" Jacob asked.

"We heard the news. We're here to celebrate," Amanda said, opening the candy jar and giving each child a sugar stick and taking one for herself.

"Don't count your chickens before they hatch," Cal Taneman said. "The bill has a long way to go. It's introduced, but it has to pass the Council, then go to the House of Representatives and pass there. Then the governor has to sign it. There are several steps with the chance of failure at each step. I have a feeling it'll be a rough battle."

"I know," said Amanda. "At least it's taken the first step. It's progress."

"If the bill passes, will you reconsider your decision to leave?" Abe McClain whispered in her ear.

The word of her leaving was getting around to all the adults. The children hadn't been told, thankfully. Amanda wasn't ready to tell them yet. She answered, "I don't know, I'll have to think about it."

"I hope you will," Abe said, "we will miss you. I heard a rumor that you might go back to Omaha to be near your aunt and uncle."

"I've thought about it, and mentioned it to Jacob and Claire."

"We will especially miss seeing you vote in a few years if the bill passes."

"I might still be in Wyoming. I haven't decided. It would be nice to be near family, but it would also be nice to be in Wyoming in case the bill passes, so I can get to see women vote for the first time." Amanda sucked her sugar stick. The thought of leaving Paradise made a sadness well up in her heart. She fought the feeling and refused to dwell on it.

Three days later, the scene was repeated. Mr. Hunter burst into the schoolroom waving a telegram, shouting, "The bill passed the Council by a vote of six to two. It goes to the House of Representatives now." Amanda and the children cheered and thanked Mr. Hunter for letting them know the news. "Are we going to go get some candy to celebrate?" the children asked.

Amanda shook her head. "Children, we need to be worried now. I expect our strongest opposition will come now. There are people in the House who hate this bill. They are, in fact, calling it a joke."

"A joke?" Marie asked, her eyes wide with surprise.

"Yes. The papers say that the bill granting women the right to vote is a joke. Most of the members of the Council and the members of the House are democrats. The rumor is, they are letting the bill go through so that it gets to the governor's desk. The governor is a republican. They think they can make a fool of the governor by giving him the ultimate decision on whether to pass the bill or not. If he passes the bill, he'll be a fool with those who don't like it. If he doesn't pass it, he'll be a fool with the people who do want it. Whatever happens, they will put him in a bad position."

"Don't they know," Ruth Henderson said, "it's not a joke to us?"

"You're right, Ruth. It's not a joke to us. The papers also say they're only passing the bill as an advertising gimmick. There are lots more men in Wyoming territory than there are women. Some people think that if they give women the right to vote, more women will want to come here to live. Then there'll be more women in Wyoming."

"Is that true?" David Henderson asked.

"I don't know. The best reason I've heard is the one that Colonel Bright, the man who introduced the bill, gave to Jacob Henderson. Colonel Bright said that his wife is educated, accomplished, and intelligent. It is only right that she has the right to vote as well as he does. That's the right reason to let women vote, because they are qualified, just as qualified as men. And they should have a right to have a voice in the laws that govern them."

"What happens to the bill now, Miss Amanda?" Zeek Henderson asked.

"Now the bill goes through the same process of discussion and voting in the House of Representatives that it went through in the Council. If it passes there, it goes to the governor to be signed."

"How long will it take?" Zeek asked.

"I don't know, we'll have to be patient and see." Amanda knew she was stepping on dangerous ground to express her political views. "We may have to wait a long time before we get any news. It could take several days before the House of Representatives acts on it. We'll have to wait." She wanted to change the subject, and said, "Tell me, what are we going to do for our Christmas party? What kind of play should we have? I was thinking about having it on December 15. Any ideas?"

"Let's do the Christmas story," little Leah said.

"That's a great idea, Leah. Any other ideas?" Everyone thought about it and didn't have any other ideas, so they agreed to do a reenactment of the traditional Christmas story. Amanda said, "I'll try to think of the best way to do it."

"We all get a part, don't we?" Leah asked.

"We all get a part," Amanda said, gently tweaking the little girl's nose. "Now, let's get ready to go home."

Amanda went to the mercantile and donned an apron. Mrs. McClain came to the counter and gave Amanda a letter to mail. Amanda canceled the stamp and went to drop it in the outgoing mailbox. Another envelope in the box caught her attention. She picked it out of the box. It was addressed to Thomas Lewellen. The return address was from Jacob Henderson.

Amanda's anger flared. She swallowed the lump rising in her throat, put the letter in her pocket, grabbed her cloak, and told her father, "I'll be back in a bit."

Ignoring the sharp air, she ran all the way to the sawmill and burst into the wood shop. "What is this?" she shouted, and threw the envelope at Jacob. "Explain it to me."

Jacob said, "It's the U.S. Mail, I have a right to write to whomever I want."

Amanda panted, trying to catch her breath. "Yes, you do. But I am your friend."

Jacob picked up the envelope from the floor. "He needs to know you're leaving."

"Jacob, please understand," she pleaded, and leaned against the workbench. "Don't write to him on my behalf. If you do, you will make me be dishonest again. I know every letter that goes out of Paradise. If you write to him again, I promise you, the letter won't leave town. It'll go straight into the fire."

Jacob put his arms around her and held her. "Amanda, Thomas should know what your plans are. He deserves to know. Don't give up on him. I think deep down in his heart, he does love you. Don't you think if he loved her, he would have been with her long before now?"

Amanda pulled away from him. "Jacob, face reality. I have! Please let it go." She opened the door, stumbled out into the blustery wind, and made her way back to the mercantile.

Not long after she got there, Jacob followed her. "Let's talk," he said.

Amanda led the way to the backroom. Jacob said, "I beg you, write to him or talk to him before you make this decision. At least clear the air between the two of you."

"If you are my friend, you won't ask this of me, Jacob."

"I won't send my letter to him. But you can't blame me for wanting to do something, anything, to keep you in Paradise, can you? Amanda, you are more than a friend. You are my children's teacher. You are my teacher. I owe you for that. I want you to be happy."

"Jacob, there is no payment due. No, wait. There is something you can do. The students are having a Christmas pageant on the fifteenth of December. We want to reenact the Christmas story. All the children will be in it. You would honor me and the school if you would agree to narrate the play for us. We will need you to read the Christmas story from the Bible."

"You honor me by asking."

"I'll let you know when the rehearsals will be."

"I will be there, and thank you. Our community is sure going to miss you when you go."

"I'll miss you. Jacob, I may need some letters of recommendation when I apply for a new job."

"You know I'll do that. I wish you would let me mail one other letter . . ."

"You stubborn old goat," Amanda said, and threw an empty box at him.

On December 6, Amanda and the children were sitting on the quilt in front of the warm potbellied stove at school talking about the play. Amanda said, "The girls can be Mary and the angels. The boys can be shepherds, wise men, and Joseph."

"How come they didn't have wise women?" Ruth Henderson asked. "Weren't women wise back then?"

"I'm sure they had women who were wise. There have always been women who were wise. They just didn't get included in this particular story," Amanda said.

"It should have wise women," Marie McClain said.

"I want to be a wise woman," Leah said.

"Me, too," said Ruth and Carrie.

"Okay. I thought for Mary and Joseph, the oldest girl and boy students in our school could do that. That means Marie and David will be Mary and Joseph, if they want to. What does every one else want to be?"

"Shepherds," the boys shouted.

"We're going to have a lot of shepherds and no angels," said Amanda.

"None of us ever claimed to be angels," said David Henderson, joking.

"I think you are all my little angels," Amanda teased. The children laughed and giggled. "This will be a wonderful play without angels and with wise women. Let's go home. Bundle up good, it's chilly today."

Amanda sent the children on their way, donned her cloak, and walked toward the mercantile. Mr. Hunter ran toward her. "It passed!" he yelled, waving his hat. "Our bill passed the House by a vote of seven to four, and goes to the governor now."

Amanda couldn't believe her ears. "For sure, Mr. Hunter?" she asked. "Do you know for sure?"

"It came over the wire. The bill was amended in the House to change the age of women who vote from eighteen to twenty-one just like for men, but it passed. Now all we have to do is wait for the governor to decide. Who knows how long it will take, but our bill made it to his desk."

They jumped up and down in the street, shouting and cheering.

That evening, Amanda sat on a stool at the counter and wrote a letter addressed to Governor Campbell, asking him to please sign the suffrage bill. She had encouraged all the adults in town to do the same. "Let the governor know how you feel," she told them. "It might help if we all write a letter."

The next day, the outgoing mailbox was stuffed with a dozen letters addressed to the governor. Amanda was thrilled when she stacked them into the outgoing mail sack, took them to the train station, and gave them to Mr. Hunter. He gave them to the conductor. The conductor climbed aboard the train and the letters chugged toward Cheyenne. *Please, Governor Campbell,* Amanda thought, watching the train disappear, *don't take it as a joke. Read our letters and know how important this is to us.*

Amanda didn't have to wait too long for an answer. On the evening of the tenth of December, she and her father were eating a late supper of chicken and dumplings. "Today was the last day of the legislative session," she said with a dismal voice, and picked at her food. "I guess the governor didn't sign the suffrage bill. I kept thinking, Mr. Hunter will come any time with some news, good or bad. But we didn't hear a single word. The bill must have died for the lack of a governor's signature. They just haven't announced it yet. Oh, well," she sighed. "It went further than I thought it would. Now maybe some other state or territory will get brave and try to pass a similar bill."

William reached across the table and squeezed her hand. "I think it will happen, eventually; if not here, somewhere else."

They cleared the dishes and food away from the

table. When her father was elbow-deep in a dishpan full of hot water and suds, they heard a heavy pounding on the door downstairs. Amanda said, "Goodness, someone must need something pretty bad. I'll see to it." She set her dishtowel on the table and hurried down the steps holding a lamp. The pounding continued. Amanda set the lamp on the counter, quickened her step, and pulled the door open.

Mr. Hunter stood on the boardwalk, his mustache bobbing, when he said, "The wires are singing tonight." He shoved a piece of paper at Amanda. She opened it and read, *Wyoming Governor Signs Suffrage Bill.* Amanda's eyes popped wide. "He signed it? He really signed it?" she shouted, and planted a kiss next to Mr. Hunter's bushy mustache.

Her father came from upstairs, asking, "What's going on down here?"

Amanda jumped into his arms, shouting, "It passed! Women in Wyoming have the right to vote!"

Amanda tingled with excitement and felt a deep relief. "It really happened! We're a part of making history." She wanted to cry, but couldn't.

Mr. Hunter gave her another hug, and said, "It's late, I'll do most of my celebrating tomorrow. Congratulations, Amanda. I know it means a lot to you." After he left, Amanda and her father blew out the lamps and went upstairs, arm in arm. Amanda leaned her head on his shoulder.

"Isn't it wonderful?" William said.

Amanda sighed. "I don't know if I'll be able to sleep tonight, I feel so giddy. I can't wait to tell the children at school. It's a wonderful victory for women everywhere, Father. At the same time, it feels a little hollow for me since I might be leaving Wyoming and going to Omaha next spring. Now, though, maybe other states and territories will follow Wyoming's lead and pass similar bills. Eventually, maybe all women everywhere will have the right to vote, too.''

"I believe that will happen," William agreed, and gave her shoulders a squeeze.

CRCRCO

Chapter 18

The school was cleaned and polished to its holiday best. All the desks were pushed against the walls. On each desk, festive candles were set in pine boughs, then lit, giving the schoolroom a bright glow and the fresh scent of mountain greenery. At the back of the room, a long table was covered with a white-lace tablecloth and filled with plates of cookies, cakes frosted with thick meringue icing, and juicy pies. A blanket was hung in the doorway between the schoolroom and cloakroom. The cloakroom served as a dressing room separating the players from the audience. Amanda stood in the cloakroom with the children gathered around her. The generous use of bed sheets, robes, towels, and blankets transformed the students into a living manger scene.

In the front of the room, on the raised platform, was a wooden cradle sitting in a generous sprinkling of straw. The best addition to their play, Amanda thought, was the piano from the saloon. Cal Taneman had loaned it to the school for their program. It had been a major undertaking for her father, Jacob, Cal, and Mr. Hunter to haul it out of the saloon, into a wagon, and up to the school. Emma Hunter was seated before it playing

Christmas carols. Amanda peeked around the curtain. Everyone in the community was packed onto the benches, waiting, quietly listening to the music.

Amanda thought, *That's what our school needs, a piano. I would work on getting one if I were going to be . . . here . . .* She let that thought linger unfinished, and turned to Jacob, who was dressed in a suit and stood by the curtain with his family Bible under his arm. "Jacob, I think we're ready. Are you ready, children?" They all looked at Amanda with eager smiles and nervous tugs on their costumes. "Okay, everybody be real quiet." Amanda walked to the front of the room, her elegant, blue, velvet gown brushing the floor. "Welcome, ladies and gentlemen, to our Christmas play. We would like everyone to help us with our play by singing 'Silent Night.' Enjoy the program."

Emma played "Silent Night." The audience sang, filling the schoolroom with music. Amanda returned to the cloakroom. As the last strains of the song died, Jacob proudly marched to the front of the room. He took his place on the platform, opened the Bible, and in a clear, deep voice, read, "And it came to pass that there went out a decree from Caesar Augustus . . . and Joseph went up out of Galilee . . . to be taxed with Mary his espoused wife, being great with child."

Amanda pointed to David, who was dressed in a robe with a towel draped over his head. He held out his elbow for Marie, who had a light-blue lace tablecloth draped around her. She held a doll wrapped in a baby blanket. Marie took David's arm. They stepped around the curtain, proceeded to the front of the room, and stepped up onto the platform.

Jacob continued, "And so it was that the days were accomplished that she should be delivered. And she brought forth her firstborn son, and wrapped him in swaddling clothes, and laid him in a manger: because there was no room for them at the inn." Marie lay the doll in the cradle, and she and David knelt. "And there were in that same country shepherds abiding in the field, keeping watch over their flock by night . . ." Amanda pointed to all her little shepherds in bathrobes, towels, and woolen blankets. They marched forward and took their places, kneeling beside the manger. Jacob read, "Now when Jesus was born in Bethlehem . . . in the days of Herod the king . . . Then Herod, when he had called the wise women . . . And he sent them to Bethlehem. . . ." Jacob interrupted himself and addressed the audience, "I want you to know, that is not a reading error. Our play, instead of wise men, has wise women."

Amanda pointed to the girls playing the wise women, and sent them forward in their colorful robes, carrying brightly-wrapped packages. They stepped up on the platform, being careful not to trip on their costumes, and set their gifts in front of the cradle before kneeling. Jacob read, "And when they were come . . . they saw the young child . . . and fell down and worshipped him: and when they opened their treasures, they presented unto him gifts: gold, and frankincense, and myrrh."

While Jacob turned the page, little Leah Henderson, with a beaming smile, spoke loud and clear, "Look, Papa, I'm a wise woman."

The members of the audience tried to stifle their laughter. Jacob lowered his voice and said, "And a fine wise woman you are, Leah." He looked at the audience and continued, "Suddenly, there was . . . a multitude of the heavenly host praising God, and saying . . ."

Amanda choked back her tears as she listened to Jacob read in his faultless voice, and thought, *He's reading with such beauty, feeling, and grace. You would think he's been reading forever. As your teacher, do you know what a gift this is to me, Jacob Henderson?*

Jacob finished, his voice resonating, "Glory to God in the highest, and on Earth, peace, goodwill toward men and women."

Emma played the piano and the children and parents filled the room with the strains of "Hark! The Herald Angels Sing."

When the song ended, all the children stood and bowed. Jacob called, "Amanda, come up here and take a bow, too." When Amanda stepped forward, everyone clapped and clapped. Amanda joined the children. The audience stood and cheered for the players. From where she stood, Amanda saw the curtain hanging between the cloakroom and the schoolroom flutter and open. Thomas Lewellen stepped around the curtain and stood, in a heavy coat, hat in hand, staring at her. She stared back, completely taken off-guard. As the crowd continued to applaud, Amanda desperately needed a breath of air, but her body refused to breathe.

Thomas took a place in the back row, nodding to those next to him. The cheering abruptly stopped, and for a moment the room was deathly quiet. Everyone stared at Thomas. Jacob regained his composure and said, "Our teacher, Miss Amanda Chappell, has some announcements."

Amanda stepped forward, her knees shaking. "Thank you for coming tonight. I regret to say, this is our last day of school until after winter break. I shall miss all of the children." Her voice faltered and wavered. "They are such wonderful children, and I have loved teaching them this term." Amanda took a deep breath and tried to gain control of herself. The children gathered around her and tried to hug her in one big mass of arms, costumes, and bodies. She forced herself not to look at Thomas and tried to pretend that he wasn't there so she wouldn't break down and cry in front of the children. She said, her voice wavering, "On each of the desks, surrounding the wall, the children have set out some of their work and papers for everyone to go around and look at. I invite you to please, do that, as they have worked very hard and done a wonderful job with their lessons. Now, some of our mothers have brought delicious refreshments. Emma Hunter has graciously agreed to play the piano. My father, William, even though he says he hasn't played for a long time and is rusty, has brought along his violin. They have offered to play some dancing music for us tonight. I thank you all for coming."

Amanda stepped from the platform. The parents gathered around her, thanking her for the wonderful program and evening. She made her way to the refreshment table where Claire was already filling cups with punch. The children ran and mobbed Thomas, trying to tell him hello. Amanda quickly stepped around the curtain, grabbed her cloak, and slipped out of the building into the clear, frosty night. The bright moon cast a bluish glow on the blanket of snow. Amanda's composure abandoned her. "Thomas Lewellen, what are you doing here?" she cried to the stars. "Why couldn't you have stayed gone forever?" Tears burned her eyes.

She entered the mercantile, turned up the lamp, and held her hands out to the warmth of the stove. Amanda wished she didn't have to go back to the school, but the large basket on the counter reminded her of the special gifts she had for the children. It was full of bright, fragrant oranges. Amanda took off her cloak, laid it over the chair, and opened the jar of sugar sticks. She counted out one for each child, putting them into the basket making sure she had one orange and one sugar stick for each child.

The bell above the door tinkled. Thomas followed her into the mercantile. Amanda's stomach lurched. *Go away, Thomas,* she thought, and remembered that while in the store, he was a customer, and deserved her courtesy. "Is there something I can get for you?"

"You can talk to me."

Her voice tensed. "I don't have time, now. They're waiting for me up at the school."

"They'll wait."

"No, they won't."

"I was just told by a school full of mad people that if I didn't march myself down here right now and talk to you, I was going to get a black eye for Christmas."

"Cal Taneman?" Amanda asked, remembering how he had punched Jacob.

"Cal Taneman, Jacob Henderson, Mr. Hunter. Worse than the threat of getting slugged by them, their wives won't speak to me or let me have any of their cookies or pie."

"The black eye would suit me just fine."

"Amanda, you don't mean that, do you?" he asked, his voice teasing.

"Yes, I do." Anger welled up in her throat. "Thomas, go away. Just go away. I have nothing to say to you." She grabbed the basket and moved away from him.

He reached for her and caught her by the wrist, causing the basket to fall. Oranges and sugar sticks rolled across the floor. Amanda struggled to escape his grasp, and screamed, "I don't want to talk to you!"

He held her tight. Through gritted teeth, he said, "Amanda, I just rode my horse through a sandstorm in Texas and two blizzards to come talk to you. And you are . . ." He grabbed her around the waist, picked her up, sat her on the counter, and held her in place. "You are going to talk to me, Amanda Chappell."

She tried to kick at him. He moved close to hold her legs still with his body. He was so near, she could smell his musky, warm scent. Amanda quit struggling and sat, feeling spent, saying, "Thomas, please don't do this. I have hurt because of you for so long. I can't do it anymore." Tears streamed down her cheeks. "Please, leave me alone."

"When I got the telegram, I came as fast as I could."

Amanda's eyes widened. "What telegram?" she asked suspiciously.

"It said, 'Amanda is leaving. If you love her, tell her to stay. Hurry.' "

"Who sent it?" she demanded.

"It wasn't signed."

"Jacob did it, I know he did. I refused to send his letter to you, but I forgot about the telegraph. Mr. Hunter could have, or . . ."

"Whoever did, I'm glad," Thomas said. "Is it true?"

"Thomas, it was so hard to be in that grader's camp with you all that time and have a crush on you and be too young for you. I was a little girl then, but now I'm a woman and it isn't any easier for me to be in Paradise with you here, too. In fact, it's harder now. Because I am old enough to understand how deep my feelings have become, and I know that you don't share them."

"Amanda, listen . . ."

"Go back to Elizabeth, whoever she is. If she rejected you, find someone else. I don't want to be your secondhand love. I want someone who wants me in the first place." She struggled down from the counter and tried to move away from him.

"Amanda . . ." He grabbed her around the waist.

She tried to squirm loose, turned, and hit him on the chest with her fists. "Let me go. Allow me a shred of dignity. Let go of . . ."

His lips found hers so fast and unexpectedly, she lost her breath. He held her tight; she tried to struggle. His firm hold on her wouldn't allow her to get free. She finally quit fighting and surrendered to the sudden kiss as waves of warmth shot through her, filling her head with a tingling numbness. Slowly, she kissed him back, answering the passion that his lips and embrace held.

When he finally let her go, tears filled her eyes. "Why did you do that?" she whispered, her voice ragged, tears rolling down her face. "I beg you, don't do that again."

He gently wiped the tears from her cheeks. "Why?"

"Don't make this any harder for me. I'm already leaving my father, a job I love, my students, Paradise, friends—don't make me have to leave the memory of your kisses, too."

Once again his lips found hers in a lingering warmth. This time she couldn't help herself, her arms wrapped around his neck, and she allowed him to kiss her even longer.

He finally pulled his lips from hers and embraced her, his arms holding her firmly. "Amanda, I'm going to kiss you until you shut up and listen to me for a minute."

Amanda gently pushed him away.

He took her hands. "I'll try to make a long story short, Amanda. First of all, Elizabeth is a very dear and good friend. We are the same age and grew up together. When my family owned slaves, she was our overseer's daughter. After I ran away, she wrote to me, saying no matter what side of the war our families were on, we were friends first. Her grandmother helped us secretly send letters back and forth. Elizabeth was, until recently, my only link to my family. She sent me news of their comings and goings and health. Even though my family no longer owns slaves, her father still works for my parents as they change their business from cotton-farming to ranching. If someone in my family or hers, other than her grandmother, had known about our letters, her father could have lost his job. She might have been disowned just like me.''

He pulled a letter from his pocket and handed it to Amanda. It was the same smeared letter from Elizabeth that Amanda had stolen. She opened it and read it again, especially the part that said, *We can still write and continue our secret relationship . . . after I'm married I can make arrangements so we can keep writing . . . Dear Thomas, I love you so . . . All my love, Your Elizabeth.*

Amanda felt herself blush. ''Thomas, I'm so s . . . sorry,'' she stammered. ''I completely misunderstood this.'' Her face felt hot. ''No wonder you shouldn't read other people's mail.''

''See that part where it says, 'I love you so?' It's true, Amanda, she does love me, and I love her. I can never repay her for the risks she took for me during the war, and these past years. But don't confuse it.''

''Confuse it?''

''It's love between good friends. You are right, Amanda. When we were in the grader's camp, you were too young, I was too young. But now, here in Paradise, we're neither one too young.''

''Why did you go away when you found out I had taken your letters?'' she interrupted.

''I had such a confusion of thoughts and feelings that I just got on my horse and rode and rode toward Texas. Partway there, I figured out what was driving me. I realized that before I think about starting a new family, I had to make peace with my old family. I decided to show up on their doorstep. If they still didn't want anything to do with me, so be it. I would then feel free to move on with my life, and Elizabeth would be free from worrying about me and my torn-up family. I figured, after all this time, I would have to be the one to reach out and try to heal the old wounds and scars.''

"What did your family say?"

"When I showed up on the porch, they were stunned. I don't think they recognized me at first. Then suddenly, my father threw his arms around me. My mother did the same, only with more tears." He continued, "My two little brothers, Shane and Michael, have grown into young men, now. It was so good to finally get to know them. It would have been a perfect reunion, except for one thing."

"What was that?"

"I was just a visitor, though a welcome one, at long last. But my home is here now, my heart is here, and the woman I hope will give me another chance to show her that I love her more than anything in the world is here."

"Thomas . . . please. My poor old heart has been through the wringer because of you."

"Listen to my plan. Do you remember how I used to like to sit and count the cattle cars coming from Omaha? Down in Texas, there are hundreds and hundreds of cattle just roaming the ranges. During the war, they got loose, ran wild, and have been breeding all along. They aren't branded and don't belong to anybody. When I saw them, I got to thinking, if we bring those cattle up here, run them on the ranges, then we can trail the beef cattle to Cheyenne to sell."

"How will you do it?"

"This spring, my two brothers and I will gather up a big bunch of those cattle and drive them up here. It'll be a long trip and a lot of work, but my brothers want to do it, so do I. We could make a lot of money. But I told them I needed to talk to you first. I would have come sooner, but Elizabeth wanted me to stay for her wedding. I owed her that, Amanda, for all she risked and did for me. As soon as the wedding was over, I came home as fast as I could. I tried to write to you.

The one letter I wrote was a terribly feeble attempt on my part, to try to let you know I was thinking of you and needed to talk to you. The things I wanted to say, I couldn't write. No matter how many times I tried, the words never came out the way I wanted them to."

"What did you want to say?"

"How I feel about you, and that I am not a railroader, a saw miller, a logger, or a builder. I'm a cowboy at heart. And if you had gone one step farther and read my response to what I thought was Elizabeth's letter, you would have read for yourself that I told her I was surprised and flattered by her letter, but that there was a woman here with beautiful red hair that I think about all the time and have come to care for with all my heart. . . ."

The bell above the door tinkled, and David Henderson stepped into the store, saying, "Everyone wants to know if you two are coming back to the party."

"David!" Amanda jumped away from Thomas, and they gathered up the spilled oranges and sugar sticks, put them in the basket, and handed it to him. "David, will you take this up to the school for me? I'll get my cloak and be right there," Amanda said, her cheeks blushing.

David snickered. "Don't worry about it. Leah was positive you would have some candy for us. Now that I have the candy, I don't think it much matters if you come back or not." He laughed and left the store with the basket.

Amanda put her hands on her hips. "Imagine that, will you? They don't care if we are at the party or not."

Thomas wrapped his arms around her, saying, "Amanda, I want to take you back to the party and be the first to dance with you. We'll have lots of time to talk about how we're going to plan the future."

Amanda said, "I want to teach for a year or two before I get married and start a family."

"That's fine with me," said Thomas. "As long as I know your heart belongs to me, and there is the matter of this letter." He pulled a piece of paper from his pocket. "I believe you wrote this." He opened her letter and held it for her to see.

She read her own words, written copying Elizabeth's handwriting. *I have loved you since I was a little girl. What do I have to do to show you? How do I find the courage to say, please love me, please marry me?* Amanda felt her face flush. "Thomas, I'm so embarrassed about that."

Thomas laughed. "If I remember right, this is the second time you've proposed to me. The first time was under a box-elder tree, along the banks of a creek. You were fourteen years old, with your glorious red hair shining in the sunlight. This letter, were it signed correctly, would be the second time you proposed to me."

Amanda felt her cheeks glow with warmth.

"I accept, Amanda, if you still want this poor old cowboy. I love you and, yes, I'll marry you, before you won't ask me again." He nuzzled her neck. "Whenever you're ready, I'll be waiting."

His lips touched hers again, only this time, she was more than willing to kiss him, and wrapped her arms around him without a single doubt in her heart.

He kissed her lips, her cheeks, her neck, then whispered, "Next time you write to me, please, sign it, With love, Amanda, not Elizabeth."

She whispered, "How about if I sign it, with *all* my love . . ."